Also by Dan Krzyzkowski

One-Lane Bridge

THE CALLER

Dan Krzyzkowski

THE CALLER

iUniverse books may be ordered through booksellers or by contacting:

iUniverse
1663 Liberty Drive
Bloomington, IN 47403
www.iuniverse.com
1-800-Authors (1-800-288-4677)

Because of the dynamic nature of the Internet, any web
addresses or links contained in this book may have changed
since publication and may no longer be valid. The views
expressed in this work are solely those of the author and do
not necessarily reflect the views of the publisher, and the
publisher hereby disclaims any responsibility for them.

Any people depicted in stock imagery provided by Thinkstock are
models, and such images are being used for illustrative purposes only.
Certain stock imagery © Thinkstock.

ISBN: 978-1-4917-6323-0 (sc)
ISBN: 978-1-4917-6324-7 (e)

Library of Congress Control Number: 2015904075

Print information available on the last page.

iUniverse rev. date: 05/05/2015

For Bernice Horvath and Karen Hessel,
two names of my past that have
helped shape my future.

Silence has a sound.

—Leslie Calloway

PROLOGUE

July 23, 1994

IT'S DIFFICULT TO KNOW where things begin sometimes. Difficult because you can't predict which way the ball is going to bounce off the events that have a way of popping up in your life. This is something I've always known, I think, but wasn't made aware of until late this afternoon, when I found the letter in my mailbox.

I'm holding the letter right now, thumbing the unopened envelope with one hand. The paper feels crisp and firm beneath my fingers. It whispers of untold secrets. The return address is some little Iowa town I've never heard of—Shellicksville.

I'm leaning back in an extendible deck chair on my back porch outside of Rocky Mount, North Carolina. Twilight is nearing, and the martins are swooping, and July surrounds me. I am cognizant of these things, in perfect tune with the present for the first time in more than six years. My right hand is clasped around a tall glass of Lipton iced tea, and I feel that too—the cold hardness of the glass and the dew that has condensed around it. Within arm's reach is a half-eaten bag of Mr. Festrada's peanuts, and I can smell the homemade aroma from that as well.

I haven't procrastinated opening the letter, nor am I apprehensive of what I may find. I've saved it for now because it's one of those things that demand a sequential, orderly mind-set, I guess. It seems heavy and potent compared to its weight in my hand, and I'd like to first be aware of where things began before taking the next step into what's yet to happen. It's tough sometimes, tracing your steps back to the starting line—it's tough knowing where things began.

But this is a major point in my life, a time in which I feel like I can belong again, and I don't wish to impose any jeopardy upon that comforting notion. Not now, after all these days and months and years. What I *can* do is take a time-out. Mr. Festrada's peanuts and the tea and the martins and the moment will wait for me, here by my chair.

As a twenty-nine-year-old single-parent mother, I don't often feel challenged to retrospect the events that have bounced the ball to where it is now, but this envelope is compelling me to do that. It seems to have gravity, seems to say things in words you don't read or hear but see in front of you.

I'm beginning to see the words now and the events they comprise. Slowly I can see more of them as the peanuts and tea and martins begin to fade. I'm *aware* of the peanuts and tea and martins fading, but that's okay because I'm allowing them to slip slowly into a suspended existence. My mellow mood is conducive to this sort of reflection, as is the evening around me.

The evening is perfect, in fact. It's one of those summer nights in which the air is pungent with deep thought.

CHAPTER 1

January 11, 1994

I REMEMBER STEALING A sip of Mary's coffee and smiling when the call came through. *The* call. It's a rare instance, two of us free in one moment, for others are always waiting to get through—especially on the 6:00 to 9:00 p.m. pull, when only six of us field the calls. Several of us, Mary and I included, had recently petitioned for an upgrade to ten—the winter season is always bad—but the installation funds weren't available.

My phone clattered at 7:42 p.m., according to my Lotensin digital desk clock, and I relished the quickening of my blood. Mary winked at me in that good-luck, good-natured way of hers from across the desk joint, and I winked back, unaware that more than seventy minutes would elapse before I next spoke to her.

My phone rang demandingly.

Music to my ears, I thought, and I picked it up.

"Hello. If you need a friend, you've called the right place," I said in my smoothest, warmest introductory voice. The answering part is critical because many have sudden second thoughts and hang up. Your greeting needs to sound welcoming and sincere. "My name is Leslie. What's your name?"

"I think there's a man in my house," a small voice replied out in the state somewhere, causing a cold feeling to pass through me.

"Did you see someone?" I asked softly. "Someone in your house?"

"No, I heard something. Down in the basement."

The voice was quivering, apparently terrified. I could tell immediately it belonged to a boy.

"Well, you can tell me what you heard if you like," I told him. It was best to avoid speaking swiftly or loudly in such situations. Best to keep the child calm, relaxed, and at ease.

"I was down … in the kitchen getting some … juice," the boy told me. He was keeping his voice low. "I was standing on a chair to get up for a glass, the one with the polkas on it 'cause it's my favorite."

"Uh-huh," I followed smoothly. "I'm listening. What happened next?"

"And I opened the door, and I was reaching up for my glass to be able to get some juice when I heard this noise downstairs."

"You heard something in your cellar, you mean?"

"Yeah. I got scared."

"What did you hear?" I asked slowly. "Or better yet, what did it sound like?"

"I don't know," he mumbled, that innocent tremor still glistening in his voice. "Like something scraping, then this bump. Like a bumping noise."

I paused for a moment—just a moment, mind you—to quickly ponder my options. Calls of this nature were the worst because you were working in an extremely gray area. Most difficult to remember is that you're here in a warm, well-lit office surrounded by a group of consenting adults, whereas the child is someplace else—a world away, for that matter. All you know is what you perceive over the phone, and that's what you have to work with. The goal is always to calm the child. More often than not, the sound is merely imagined. It's amazing, some of the noises kids claim to hear when they're alone in a big house. Every noise known to man is threatening to a latchkey child. It's simply a matter of ensuring the caller that the house was most definitely creaking with age or shifting on a gust of wind.

But as a volunteer, it is always your duty to field the calls objectively. Bad things do happen on occasion. Thus belies the gray area. Heck, some hear nothing at all but use it as an excuse to call and talk with someone. That's how lonely some of these children are—believe me. A girl named Samantha rang in one night to report some disturbing sounds coming from the attic above her bedroom. "It sounds like someone is playing hopscotch up there," were the words she used if my memory serves. We spoke for more than thirty minutes. Near the end of our talk, she confessed to there being nothing at all—she was lonely and wanted someone to talk to. Her parents had gone to the movies and left her alone. She was six years old.

But the coin always has two sides, something we volunteers mustn't forget. Samuel Evans, the burly man in the far corner right now, received a call several months ago from a nine-year-old boy who insisted his house was being robbed. The boy had locked himself in his sister's bedroom, terrified. He was in tears and on the verge of hysteria when he called. Sam was incredible that night. In all my twenty-eight years, I don't believe I've known a man who possesses as deep-rooted a compassion for others, children in particular. And that includes my late husband. Anyway, Sam instructed the boy to stay put and talked him through it until his parents returned home an hour later. The prowler was gone by then, as was $24,000 worth of jewelry from the master bedroom, two doors down from the sister's room where the boy had endured the scare.

"What's your name?" I asked.

"Justin," he replied weakly.

"Justin, are you home by yourself tonight?"

"Uh-huh."

Of course he was alone. He wouldn't have called otherwise. But I needed to know for certain.

Mary smiled at me from across our desk, gesturing to her empty mug. I shook my head.

"Where are your parents, Justin? Do you know where they went?"

"No. They said they were going out, be back later."

"When did they leave?" I asked.

"Don't know. An hour ago, maybe."

"Did they say when they would return?"

"Uh-uh."

Did they say anything at all? Did they give you a hug before they left? Did they tell you to behave?

Well, that closed the door on one thing. Contacting the parents was out of the question. Most parents at least left their children with a name and number, a place to call in the event of an emergency.

By policy, we were forbidden to dial the police. There were various reasons for this, none more controversial than Provision 10-93, which I'll address in time. The best we could do was exhort the child into breaking the connection and dialing 911 him- or herself, something many shied away from out of fear of their parents' reaction. "My mom'll get mad at me if I do that," one girl explained, calling for her younger brother, who had somehow gotten his arm caught in the kitchen-sink garbage compactor. I coaxed her into at least calling a neighbor, who dialed 911. Paramedics and police arrived within minutes. They spent three hours extricating the boy's right hand from the jaws of the kitchen sink. The boy lost the top tri-portion of his middle finger in the bargain.

"How old are you, Justin?"

"Seven."

"Whoa, you're getting up there, aren't you? Before you know it, you'll be man of the house."

An impish moan was the only reply, replete with implications that being man of the house wasn't the least bit appetizing at the time.

"Any brothers or sisters, Justin?"

"Uh-uh. Just me. I'm scared. There's a man in my house—I know it."

"Okay, Justin, I believe you. And I'm on your side. But you have to listen to me, okay?"

"Uh-huh."

"Where in the house are you right now? Are you in a safe place?"

At the very least, I hoped Justin had gotten out of the kitchen. Most doors leading down into basements were located either in the kitchen or in an adjacent hall.

"Upstairs," he answered softly. In my head, I saw him peering around anxiously. I felt the childlike dread pounding through his veins. I sensed the iciness in his belly. "I'm in my parents' room, under the bed."

"Good," I said, commending him on his thoughtfulness. A child's typical response to hearing strange noises is to freeze. Justin had conjured the will to act. He'd climbed down from his chair and crept up the stairs to his parents' room, where he knew he could both hide and phone simultaneously.

"I'm on the cordless phone," he told me.

"It was very smart of you, Justin, to think of calling us. That was very good. Now tell me—can you see out from under the bed?"

"Yeah. The bedroom door is open, and I can see down the hallway," he said. "The steps are down at the end. That's where I came up."

"Okay, good. Very good. That hallway is empty now, right?"

"Uh-huh," he replied, but not without the fright implicit in the notion that he'd *be able* to see the intruder enter the hall via the staircase if the scenario presented itself.

"Can you hear anything, Justin? Anything at all?"

"No. It's all quiet now."

It must be terrifying, an empty house like that. Everything's a threat now. Every little tweak in the floor will send a shudder up that boy's spine.

"You can't hear anything? Not even those noises from the basement?"

"Nope."

Though only several minutes old, we'd reached a critical point in the conversation. As the volunteer, the one being relied upon, I had to decide how to approach the problem and what action to suggest. We were still in the gray area. All I knew was what I heard. Sure, I could *assume* Justin had heard the house shifting on its foundation … but it was *he* who'd heard the sound, not me.

You don't know anything yet, my inner voice asserted. *For now, you need to play along with him. The boy is scared, and that's why he called. It's your job to make him feel safe. You've done this before, Leslie.*

"All right, Justin, this is what I want you to do," I said, speaking slowly and clearly. "What I want is for you to actually do nothing at all. I want you to stay right where you are. Can you do that for me?"

"Uh-huh," he replied, with a nervousness that suggested he had no intentions of moving to begin with.

"I want you to stay where you are 'cause it sounds like you're safe there. I'll stay on the phone with you. If you hear anything more from downstairs, let me know, okay?"

"Yeah. There isn't anything now, but I know he's there 'cause I heard him. I know I did." His voice shook.

It wasn't my place to dial the police—Teri Wainwright would have my body on a skewer—but sooner or later, something was going to have to give. *Don't even think about it, Leslie. Don't you dare.*

I asked, "Do you have a good next-door neighbor you can call, Justin? Someone you know?" I was aware, of course, that Justin would need to know the neighbor's phone number by heart—sneaking out to locate a phone book was surely not an option.

"I tried already," he said, "before I called you. They're not home."

"There wasn't any answer?"

"Uh-uh. No one was home."

"Are there any other neighbors you can call, then?"

"No, they're the closest ones."

"You don't know anyone else close by?"

"Uh-uh."

Well, so much for that idea. Even had Justin known some of the other neighbors around him, I doubted the likelihood of his having those numbers memorized as well.

Another thought occurred to me, and I wondered what his address might be. It was another policy, to preserve our anonymity as well as that of our callers, not to ask for addresses. But what if something happened during our conversation? What if the intruder was real? What if Justin was discovered, and the line was to suddenly go dead?

For the first time that evening, I reached down into my purse, feeling around for my car phone. My fingers found it easily enough. I wouldn't use it, of course—*couldn't* use it—but knowing it was there did impart a small measure of comfort.

CHAPTER 2

SOME WORDS ABOUT 10-93.

That's what *we* called it, anyway—those of us who know the difference between a social service and a social suction cup. It refers to an inauspicious series of events that occurred in October of '93, a little more than three months ago.

It happened during an afternoon shift. One of our most experienced volunteers, an older woman named Joan Baskely, fielded a call around two o'clock from a young boy who had accidentally set his house on fire. The boy had been in his backyard burning leaves. Things had gotten out of control. In a matter of minutes, a sizeable portion of his yard was in flames. By the time he dashed inside to pick up the phone, flames were creeping up the wood siding along the back of the house.

Joan scribbled the boy's address onto a slip of paper, advised him to leave the house immediately, and then hung up and dialed 911. Sheldon's finest were dispatched without a moment's waste.

The only problem was that the call was bogus. A pair of teens who had decided to cut school that day had made the prank call from a pay phone not five blocks from the church in which our help center is located. It very nearly turned out to be the worst mistake of their lives.

Eight minutes after the local dispatcher received Joan Baskely's call, a second call came in from the other end of town, south of Forest Glen Road. The difference was that this fire was real. The Tiny Tots Nursery School was in flames. Forest Glen Road is nine miles cross-town from the false address provided by the pranksters. As a result, the tankers were delayed an estimated four minutes. It was during this time that a four-year-old girl named Natalie Harris came close to losing her life. She spent five days in County Hospital due to severe smoke inhalation.

It was the two teens who had cried wolf, but it was the helpline that took the fall. Our funds plateau at six thousand dollars a year—all from public donations. When word of what had happened got out, we came close to losing half of them. Teri Wainwright, our acting chair, had to wage a PR war with the local press to preserve our image. Soon afterward, in a closed-doors meeting with all twenty-one volunteers, Teri announced that absolutely no 911 calls were to be placed out of our office … at least until things cooled down.

Two months passed without further incident … until a Wednesday evening in mid-December, a week before Christmas. It was I who received a call from a little girl—crying hysterically and borderline incomprehensible—who told me that her mom and dad were having a really bad fight. I heard, in the background, a high-strung male voice screaming at a quailing female voice. I also heard household items being knocked around, possibly being broken. "Do you know what your address is?" I asked the girl. "Can you tell me where you live?"

She lived at 6 Cider House Lane. "Please do something, lady. Please help before my dad does something really bad to my mom."

I told her to run into the bedroom and hide in the closet. Help was coming. Then I broke the connection and dialed

911. I became the first volunteer at our small outfit to break the 10-93 lockdown.

When I returned to the church two nights later for my ensuing shift, Teri Wainwright caught me by the elbow and led me into her office. I went willingly, expecting to receive some form of verbal praise for having had the guts to do what I'd done.

Instead, Teri began pacing back and forth behind her desk, one hand pressed to the side of her head, massaging her temple.

"I heard about what happened the other night," she said. "I listened to the playback."

I said nothing. I stood in front of the oatmeal-colored sofa, watching Teri carefully.

"The parents of the girl who called … the ones having the argument?" She stopped walking and looked at me. "Do you know who they were?"

"It's none of my business who—"

"The husband's name is Donald Underwood. Does that ring a bell?"

"I've never heard of him."

Teri resumed her pacing. She sighed. Finally, she palmed one hand against the front of her face and then muttered through her splayed fingers, "He's a top executive for Raymond and Brian Achulsen."

I suddenly felt my legs going weak in the knees. I sank slowly onto the oatmeal-colored sofa.

The Achulsen Bros., Inc. was a bioengineering and biotechnology research facility, privately owned and funded, built on a four-hundred-acre estate here in Sheldon. They were also our number-one donor each year.

"I understand, Leslie," Teri said, "that you had no way of knowing who the girl's parents were. But for God's sake, we were under a 911 lockdown. Did I not make it clear—"

"That was two months ago. I think things have cooled down sufficiently—"

"I'll be the judge of that!" she cried. "Christ, Leslie, we're a low-budget outfit here—our money doesn't fall from the sky. Need I remind you what happens on April first of every year? Brian Achulsen, accompanied by a small media entourage, drives over here himself to hand-deliver a check in the amount of three thousand dollars—50 percent of our annual lifeline. We lose it, Leslie, and we are *under*."

I held out both arms, palms up. "What you're saying, Teri, is that we're a lame duck social service. We're like a fire department with all the bells and sirens but no water to pump through the hoses."

She pointed at me with a menacing stare. "You *know* how rare it is for us to get calls of high emergency. Most of our callers are just lonely kids who—"

"Easy for you to say, Teri—you're not over there manning the lines." I stood and moved toward the door. "It's easy to wear glass slippers when you aren't the one who has to run across granite flagstones."

As I reached for the knob to pull the door open, Teri stepped forward and grabbed my arm.

"I'm sorry, Leslie. I'm sorry it has to be this way. I know …" She bit her lip. "I know how dedicated you are, considering all that you've been through, but …"

"But?"

She lowered her gaze to the floor, sighed, and then met my eyes. "Look, there's only a slim chance that Underwood will learn that the 911 call originated from our office. But I'm not taking any chances. And for now, I'm keeping this little discussion between the two of us. All right?"

"All right. And next time, maybe their argument will escalate, and he'll take her head off with his hunting rifle. I just hope it's not me, Teri, who has the misfortune of doing nothing to prevent it."

As I started to pull the door open, Teri tightened her grip on my arm and said, "I admire your determination, Leslie. I always have. But I cannot afford to have loose cannons in here that might jeopardize our purpose. There are boys and girls out there who depend on us every day." Teri paused. Speaking slowly, she added, "If you get into trouble again, Leslie, I'm going to have to dismiss you. I'm sorry."

"I'm sorry too, Teri." I walked out of her office.

And now you know the predicament in which I found myself when, three weeks later, a terrified, little boy dialed in during one of the worst winter storms in this town's recent memory, claiming that a dangerous man had broken into his house … and my hands were tied behind my back.

And that was only the start of it.

CHAPTER 3

WE TALKED FOR A while. It was nice to slip into the shelter of conversation.

I asked Justin what he liked to do. Make models, he said—which was wonderful, I told him. My cousin had always loved to build warplanes with my father when I was a kid. Justin also enjoyed video games on Nintendo. Blades of Steel and Mega Man Three were his favorites. He liked to draw pictures of dogs and horses. I asked if he had a dog. He said he didn't. I detected a sad tone in his voice, which conveyed, I thought, a pervasive loneliness. This was typical of our daily callers. Our Call-A-Friend station was based in Sheldon, Connecticut. Although our radius of call-ins extend as far north as Danbury and as far east as Milford, most come directly from the town of Sheldon and its outlying districts. Additional help centers are based out of other cities across the state—Waterbury, Hartford, and New Haven, to name a few—but nowhere is a helpline for latchkey kids more needed than it is here. Sheldon is a bustling hive of middle- and upper-middle-class households, many of which include two working parents. It's a town of professionals, scientists, entrepreneurs, and PhDs, many of whom travel and work long hours. Some employ babysitters or nannies to look after their children. Some implore their children to look after themselves.

Being a latchkey child poses many problems. Eighty percent of our callers cite loneliness as their worst adversary. They stream home from school every day to be confronted by an empty house—no mom to greet them at the door or hug them or ask them how their day went. Many will tune out their listlessness with video games or television. I received a call from a boy not long ago who had no real friends in whom to confide after school other than his dog, Mickey. Both parents worked until six o'clock every night. Mickey had been the lad's best friend, pulling and jumping against his chain as the boy stepped off the school bus each day. They played keep-away with a tennis ball in the backyard. The boy was sobbing miserably when I answered the phone that afternoon. He was calling to tell someone that he'd found Mickey lying dead in the grass behind the doghouse. He was upset and needed someone to talk to. I spent nearly twenty minutes on the phone with him. I told him Mickey was in a better place, free of pain and suffering. I reminded him of the happiness he had brought into Mickey's life, and vice versa. I told him that all living things must one day stop living, including those closest to us. I may have added that grief, in the end, is often the price to be paid for love.

*   *   *

"So, what happened in school today?" I asked, remembering the importance of conversation. You can't just raise your hand and land a seat in this place. You're required to undergo two weeks of basic training—how to assuage frightened callers, entertain the bored ones, and how best to speak to the lonely. Each of us has at arm's length a copy of *Ten Thousand and One Ribrackers for Kids*. My copy was nestled into the far corner of my desk, forgotten.

Silence on Justin's end. I heard static but nothing else.

"Justin? Justin, are you there?"

"I heard him," he whispered. "He's downstairs. I heard him, he's down—"

"Okay, Justin, okay—"

"He's there, I know it, I know—"

"Justin, calm down. I believe you." I tried to keep my voice at a minimum. "Just relax, all right? Can you relax for me?"

"I think so, yeah."

"You're in a safe place, remember. Just keep your voice low and stay where you are. I'm right here, okay? I'm right here with you."

"Okay."

"Now tell me what you heard. What did it sound like?"

"It was a door opening. It was the basement door. I know it."

That rattled me. Houses *did* creak and moan but not in a manner resembling the sound of a door opening. It took a person to open a door.

"Where is the basement door, Justin? Is it in the kitchen?"

"Yeah, across from the counter. I heard it open." He was still whispering, which seemed instinctive.

"Do you hear anything now?" I asked him. "Do you hear someone moving around down in the kitchen?"

"No. But I know I heard the door open down there. I know I heard it."

"It's okay, Justin, I believe you. Just do what I say, all right?"

"Uh-huh."

My quickening pulse was enough to tell me we were leaving the gray area and entering the black. Justin, left home alone by his parents, was caught in the middle of a home invasion.

"Stay put and keep your voice as low as you can. If you hear anything else—and I mean anything at all—you tell me. Are we clear?"

"Uh-huh."

On a whim, I asked him, "Was it snowing before, Justin? When you last looked out the window, had the snow started?"

"Yeah."

"Was it snowing hard?"

"Uh-huh. Real hard."

"Well, it's a good bet you won't have school tomorrow." This elicited an indifferent moan, and I realized that school was probably a salvation for Justin, a place to be around other kids. A cancellation, on the other hand, would translate into an entire day alone in the house.

I can't see outside from where I am now. Our windowless office is embedded in the basement of the Reformed Church at the intersection of Main and Fifth. Every winter, we get hit with one or two nor'easters. One of these had been forecast to sweep through tonight and into tomorrow. Six to seven inches were expected, with gusting winds. The storm's preface had greeted me upon my arrival here tonight as the first minute flakes had begun spiraling down from the hard, slate sky.

Apparently, the snow had picked up since then. Had this been a business, we'd have called it a day and closed early. But we weren't here to make a presentation or close a deal. We were here voluntarily. An inch of snow or six feet of it, there were kids out there who needed us.

That half-a-foot forecast swam through my head again, however, and I considered my chances of making it home that night. Patrick wasn't alone. Tammy—my sitter—was with him, but she was only sixteen, and likely mulling over the same predicament.

That's for later, I knew. *You have other business at hand here. Keep your head in the game, Leslie.*

"Tell me, Justin: are there any outside doors that go into your basement? Like a garage door?"

"Yeah. The storm doors."

I knew what he was speaking of. Bilco doors, which opened at a diagonal alongside the house.

The evidence I had was enough to suggest that everything Justin had said was true. I thought about inquiring whether or not the Bilco doors had been locked, but this seemed irrelevant and an invitation to panic. What I really needed was to assume a stand on the situation. I needed to establish some form of order and structure ... but the snowstorm came back and bit me, giving rise to a new quandary: "Justin, didn't your parents know it was going to snow tonight?" It was a question that only deepened the mystery of their departure. After all, what could be so important to risk an approaching nor'easter with a seven-year-old child alone in the house at night?

"Yeah, but my dad has chains on his wheels," Justin answered. Which meant that Mom and Dad had been bent on braving the weather either way.

The absence of windows in our office lent power to my imagination. In my mind's eye, I saw the blowing snow drifting higher and higher, burying roads and driveways. My Bronco had four-wheel drive, but how deep would the snow be come nine o'clock tonight? The mother in me drummed at the need to call home and assure Tammy that things were okay and not to worry.

Relax, Leslie. Tammy will be fine. She knows you'll be on the phone all night. Besides, they probably have those plows out by now, so there's no need to waste—

"I heard him again," Justin whispered suddenly.

I paused before asking, "What did it sound like?"

"A drawer. He opened a drawer. Down in the kitchen."

"Are you sure?"

"Uh-huh, yeah." His voice trembled.

"I know you're scared, Justin, but you need to relax for me, okay? You must relax. I'm right here with you."

"Uh-huh."

"Continue whispering like you are now. If he's making as much noise as you say he is, then he must think the house is empty. He probably thinks you aren't home, that you went out with your mom and dad. As long as he doesn't know you're there, we have the advantage. We just have to keep it that way. And you need to be relaxed, right?"

"Yeah," he replied. "He just closed the drawer down there."

I believed him now. I believed everything he'd told me. It wasn't just one thing but the merging of all the elements. The veracity of the fear in his voice, the sequence of events and how he described them had all the trappings of reality.

Then a new thought occurred to me. According to the boy, the intruder was down in the kitchen. But where might he wind up? *Not in the sunroom checking out the perennials and biennials, I don't think. And not in front of the television watching* Monty Hall *reruns, either. He'll be on his way up the stairs, Leslie. And after that …*

The master bedroom. I couldn't help but think back to Sam's call, the boy who'd hung low in his sister's bedroom while the twenty-four grand of jewelry had been lifted from the parents' room.

Which was precisely where Justin was now, as we spoke. The intruder was in the kitchen, but the master bedroom was a certain stop along the way. How would the boy react? And what of the cordless phone? Didn't some models have that little red light that lit up when the receiver was removed from the cradle? Would the intruder see it? Might he waltz into the master bedroom confident he was alone, then stop dead in his tracks when he saw the cordless housing on the nightstand with the phone missing and the little red light on?

So many questions, Leslie, but so little time in which to ask them. You know what has to be done now, don't you?

"Okay, Justin, enough is enough. I want you to sit tight while I dial the police." I held my car phone in my free hand, keeping it below the desktop to keep it hidden. "Do you know your address, Justin?"

"Um ... uh ... my what?"

"Do you know the name of the street you live on?"

"Uh ... it's ... I don't ... I'm not sure."

He either doesn't know it or he's too damned scared to remember it. What are you gonna do now, Leslie?

"How 'bout your phone number, Justin? Do you know your phone number?"

"Um, it's ... it's ..."

"Relax and take a breath. It might even be written on the inside of the phone, right above the buttons."

"It's 724 ... uh, 8159."

"Okay ... good." I jotted down the number on a slip of scratch paper as I dialed 911 on my private phone. "Hold still, Justin, I'm calling the police now."

Teri can take her ultimatums and go to hell, I thought, waiting as the line rang in one ear. It rang four, five, six times, until finally an automated female voice clicked on: "All lines are currently busy. Please try your call later."

This was followed by the dry click of a disconnect.

I sat perfectly straight in my chair, the car phone held absently to one ear, immersed in a stunned semistupor. *All lines are currently busy? How can 911 possibly be busy?*

Another voice, one that was cool, calculating, and a little bit frightening: *The storm. Something's happened, somewhere. Some major event or catastrophe, and everybody's calling to report it, and the lines are log-jammed.*

I had to resolve myself to remain calm. I'd give it another ten minutes and then try again. In the meantime, there was

still the matter of Justin hiding in the master bedroom …
what was now a potentially dangerous location.

"Are the police coming? Are they coming, Leslie?"

"Soon, Justin, very soon. But listen, we're gonna need to
get you to a safer place than where you are right now. Okay?"

"Why?" he asked, with a notable rise in his voice. No
doubt, moving from beneath that bed was the last thing in
the world that boy wanted to do.

"You have to trust me on this, Justin. I'll be here with
you the entire time. I'm just afraid that man might come into
your parents' room, so I think we should move you before he
gets there. Is he still down in the kitchen?"

"I don't know. I can't hear anything now." His whisper
was fearfully unsteady.

"What I need you to do very quietly is tell me about the
upstairs of your house. What can you see from where you
are? Can you see the hall at all?"

"Uh-huh, all the way."

"You can see down to the end of the hallway?"

"Uh-huh."

"From under that bed?"

"Uh-huh."

"Tell me, Justin, where are the stairs? How far down the
hall are they?"

"The end," he replied. "I already told you."

"The stairs are all the way at the end? At the end of the
hall?"

"Yeah, but there's more stairs in my room. Round ones
that go down to the den."

This came as a surprise. Another staircase?

"You have stairs in your room too?"

"Yeah, round ones."

A spiral staircase, from Justin's room going down
to the den. I doubted the boy knew how crucial that
information was.

"Where is your room, Justin? If you're looking down the hall right now, which door is yours, and which side is it on?"

"First one on the left. That one's mine. Then a bathroom and a study."

"The bathroom and study are on the left side also?"

"Yeah."

"How 'bout the right side, Justin? What rooms are on the right side of the hall?"

"A guestroom, then a big closet."

"And the stairs are at the end?"

"Uh-huh. On the right."

Too many words were soaring through me for me to process at once. That spiral staircase in Justin's room. More importantly, his was the first room on the left. Conceivably, the boy would only be exposed in the hallway for a few seconds before he could slip into his room and hide. When the perpetrator came up the main stairwell, Justin could slink down into the den and get out of the house.

But what if the perp came up the spiral staircase into Justin's room? And how wise was it to instruct the boy to step into the hall?

As if reading my thoughts, Justin said: "I could go through the alley too."

"The alley? What is that?"

"Through my mom and dad's bathroom, into the guestroom."

"Hold up, Justin. Where is your mom and dad's bathroom? Do they have a bathroom on the right side of their bedroom?"

"Yeah, it's the alley."

Now I understood. The alley. On the right side of the master bedroom was a bathroom that also connected with the guestroom—first room on the right. It suddenly made sense. Justin could slip through the bathroom and into the guestroom without ever stepping foot into the hall.

But where would that leave him? A dead end?

"So, what you're saying is that you can get to the guestroom without going into the hallway. Right?"

No response.

"Justin?"

No response.

Keep your voice down. Don't panic him.

"Justin, what's wrong?"

"I heard him again. He broke something."

"What did he break?"

"I don't know," he answered unsteadily. "Something glass. He broke it real loud. I'm scared, I'm really—"

"Okay, Justin, I know. I know you're scared. I'm scared too, but I'm right here with you. What you need to do is take a deep breath. Can you do that?"

I heard him inhale, exhale.

"Where did the sound come from?"

"I think the dining room. It's closer than the kitchen."

I knew what he meant by that. The dining room was closer to the main stairwell than the kitchen.

"Okay, you told me you could get to the guestroom through the alley, right?"

"Yeah."

"Is there another round set of stairs in there or something? Is there another way to get downstairs through the guestroom?"

"No, there's a window."

"There's a window in the guestroom?"

"Yeah."

"Can you climb out of it and get to the ground safely?"

"I can go down the web, but I don't have shoes or socks on, and Daddy'll get mad."

I didn't have to think long on that one. The web, a trellis. Free and clear of vines this time of year.

"Have you climbed down the web before, Justin? Have you ever done it before?"

"Yeah, in the summer, but I got punished."

"Well, you won't get punished now, Justin, believe me. If there's someone in your house and you need to get out, your mom and dad will be proud when they find out you climbed down the web. I'll even talk to them if you want."

"You will?"

"I promise."

"But it's snowing, and I have bare feet."

I had to stop and think about that. Maybe spidering down the trellis wasn't such a hot idea. If the boy fell and injured himself, Teri would come after me with an elephant gun. The helpline itself might incur legal difficulties. And the shame and guilt I experienced for encouraging Justin to make such a bold maneuver would be overwhelming.

But what were my options? That boy *had* to get out of the house.

"Do you think you can get to the neighbor's house once you reach the ground, Justin? I know it'll be real cold on your feet, but is the house close enough?"

"But there's no one home there," he insisted, alluding to his phone call prior to this one.

"We may have to take that chance. You could probably get in somehow. If not, run to someone's driveway and sit in their car. We just have to get you out of there. You understand?"

"I think."

"Okay, one more thing before we do this. Listening, Justin?"

"Yeah," he whispered softly.

"I don't want you to talk to me during the entire time it takes you to walk from your parents' room over to the window in the guestroom, okay?"

"Uh-huh."

"I want you to be as quiet as you can, which means you can't talk at all. What I'll do so we can keep communicating is ask yes or no questions only. Do you understand, Justin?"

"I think."

"If I ask you a question while you're moving and the answer is no, then tap the mouth part of the phone once. If the answer is yes, tap it twice. You got it?"

"Uh-huh. So I don't have to talk."

"Right. Use a fingernail to tap the receiver, but tap it lightly, just enough so that I can hear it, okay?"

"Yeah."

The wind seemed to have died out of his voice, his words coming through all breathless and constricted.

"Is everything quiet right now?"

A pause. His world of silence and stealth was a light fuzz of static to me. It was then I realized that silence has a sound—a sound unlike any other. Try sitting in your basement in the dead of night when you're home alone. I guarantee you'll hear everything: the subtle clicks in the ceiling, the scuttling of thousand-legged bugs over the concrete walls … and perhaps some sounds that *don't* exist. Yes, I am a firm believer now. Silence has a sound.

"I think so, yeah."

"You don't hear anything? Anything at all?"

"No," he whispered.

"Okay, that's good," I told him. I wanted to be sure the intruder wasn't in the process of creeping up the stairs as Justin crawled out from his hideout … though a darker, deeper part of my mind insisted I had no way of knowing that for sure.

"Just relax, Justin. Everything'll be fine. I'm right here with you."

"Okay. Should I go now?"

Now or never, a voice inside me said.

"Yes. Crawl out slowly and quietly to the right side, closest to the alley. Then tiptoe into the bathroom and stop when you get there. Okay, go."

For several seconds I heard the loose rustling of bed sheets as the boy rolled to his right and into the clear. The rustling ceased, and I knew he was into the open. Exposed.

It's hard to explain this as I felt it, but I seemed to be living this vicariously, seeing everything as it transpired through a gaping eye in my mind. I envisioned rolling out from under that king-sized bed—an awful moment of vulnerability as I snapped my head around, searching for alien movement. And then getting to my knees and tottering slowly to my feet, my heart throbbing as my eyes found the open doorway, expecting a slovenly vagrant to be standing there, watching me with bulbous and luminescent eyes.

"We're on the tap system now, remember," I reminded him. "Everything okay so far?"

Tap-tap. Yes, everything was okay.

"Into the bathroom," I instructed him. "Just relax. It's your house, remember. You know your house better than he does."

At least, that's what we're assuming.

I chose to ignore that voice.

"Are you in the bathroom now, Justin?"

Tap-tap. Yes, in the bathroom.

"All right, this is what I want you to do. Just hold still and listen for a minute. Make sure everything's quiet before you go on."

I paused, listening to the static of my world as Justin listened to the silence of his. I heard a countless array of imaginary noises amid that phone fuzz. A chair sliding out, a door creaking open … a footstep. Silence has a sound.

"Do you hear anything?"

A pause.

Tap-tap. Yes, he heard something. My pulse rate jumped a notch.

"Does it sound like it's coming from downstairs?" I asked.

Tap-tap. Yes.

That was good. But I could only wonder how much longer until the intruder moved up the stairs.

"Do you feel all right, Justin? Ready to move again?"

Tap-tap.

Good. Ready to move.

"I don't want you to close any doors as you go, Justin. All right? Be as quiet as you can. You with me?"

Tap-tap.

"Okay, you're in the bathroom still. You're in the alley. Is the door from the bathroom to the guestroom open ahead of you?"

Tap-tap.

"Good. Tell me, Justin, are any lights on in the guestroom?"

Tap. No, none on.

"Good. It's better if it's dark."

My heart was speeding up now; I could feel it knocking up the pace the closer we got to the window. To the trellis. The ticket down, the way out. From there to a neighbor's house. I had to force myself to remain calm and patient. I had to restrain the urge to rush to the window and scamper for dear life. Making haste would incite panic, I knew, especially for a seven-year-old.

"This is what I want you to do, Justin. Are you listening?"

Tap-tap.

"I want you to stay in the bathroom, but right at the edge, so you can peek your head around into the guestroom. Can you do that for me?"

Tap-tap.

I waited for a moment, during which I saw myself craning my neck around that bulwark to inspect the darkness. Phantom shadows seemed ready to leap out of every corner.

"Is the door from the guestroom to the hallway open?"

Tap-tap. Yes.

"Is it all the way open? Like wide open?"

A short pause.

Tap.

"Is it halfway open?"

Tap.

"Just a little bit open?"

Tap-tap.

The door was ajar. I saw that slice of hallway through that Cyclopean eye of mine ... and in my imagination, saw a shrouded figure moving suddenly past it, blocking out the dim light. I shuddered. And I was inside a church.

Be strong, Justin. We'll get through this.

"Everything okay so far, kid?"

Tap-tap.

"Hear anything?"

Tap.

Good. Nothing.

"Okay, I think we're ready, but listen up first. Here's the plan. You listening?"

Tap-tap.

"First things first, Justin. Be as quiet as possible opening the window. When you get it open, climb out slowly, quietly, and *carefully*. Whatever you do, don't hurry. Drop the phone into the snow on the ground and climb down slowly. We'll probably lose our connection when the phone hits the ground, so I'll hang up over here. Don't call me back right away; it'll just waste time. You need to get to a warm place as quickly as possible. Just get to a neighbor's house, anyplace with lights on. When you get there, I want you to call me right back, okay? All right? Can you do all that?"

A hesitation, as if considering.

Tap-tap.

"Okay, then. I'm ready when you are. Let's do this. Move quietly across the room and do your thing."

My mind's eye took over. Though I'd never seen this guestroom before in my life, I envisioned a queen-sized bed and saw myself shuffling nervously around it, peeking over my shoulder at that crack in the door, that chasm of hallway. I felt my blood gathering speed with every step toward the window, snow crusting about the edges and a hard wind whipping by; never had a Connecticut storm sounded so sweet and so free. I felt the edges of that window in my hands, the phone tucked tightly between shoulder and ear as I slid the panes to one side … the snow rushing in, an Arctic blast blowing past me. Pausing for just a second as I locked my eyes onto the welcoming lights of neighboring houses, glowing distantly but invitingly—beacons of hope in a world of sudden chaos. Then crawling out and over the sill, the exhilaration of the action itself. Dropping the phone into the snow.

But I wasn't in that house. I was here, at the intersection of Main and Fifth, all cute and warm and snuggled in the church basement. All I heard was silence, and it was the deep chill of that silence that made me realize I *had* been waiting for something, something all along. A soft bump or a clatter. Or the window being moved aside, and then winter's blizzardy breath roaring past the receiver, and the phone dropped to the ground—the click of a broken connection.

But I heard none of those things. I heard nothing but silence. That deep, beckoning, apathetic phone fuzz. Silence has a sound. And that sound was now telling me something was very wrong.

"Have you gotten the window open?"

A pause.

Tap.

Did he hear something else? Footsteps making their way up the stairs, maybe? Or some other noise that has him frozen in terror?

I opened my mouth to inquire about the possible noises—footfalls up the stairs, perhaps. And then it hit me with a shameful weight. I cursed myself for failing to foresee.

"Is the window stuck, Justin? Is it stuck?"

That's what I saw in the silence now. A boy of seven struggling to move something. Something that wouldn't go. And trying equally hard to maintain his silence.

Tap-tap.

Of course. The window was frozen shut.

CHAPTER 4

LIVING JUSTIN'S EXPERIENCE VICARIOUSLY was worse, I decided, than had I been there myself. I had to this point made all the major decisions, including orchestrating Justin's movements. But we had reached a point at which I could do no more. I can't say for sure what I would've done had it been me in that house instead of a seven-year-old boy ... but I can guess. Panic would have overwhelmed me. I would have struggled harder, grappling with that window regardless of the commotion it made. I would have forced it open on pure adrenaline, then thrown myself out to the trellis, scampering to the ground like a squirrel dashing down a tree.

But I had to keep my emotions under control. I wasn't the one in that house, and I couldn't transfer my strength into Justin's arms. I could *tell* him what to do, but no more. It was a powerless feeling.

I asked, "The window's frozen, isn't it?"

Tap-tap.

Keep your voice low, Leslie. Low and steady.

"Justin, I don't want you to touch the window anymore," I told him levelly. "It'll make too much noise to get it open if it's really stuck. Is everything okay? Are you all right?"

No response. No tap.

I waited, listening to my pulse thump against the edge of the phone. The plastic handle was damp with perspiration.

"Justin? Are you okay?"

I waited. Waiting, waiting …

Be patient. He's probably moving.

No response.

My heart picked up the pace. I didn't like this at all.

Waiting, waiting …

He'll answer, he'll answer …

Bullshit. Something was wrong. I couldn't help but raise my voice.

"Justin? Justin, what is it? What's wrong?"

Come on, kid, answer me. Answer me …

"Justin? Justin, tell me—"

That's not a yes or no question, Leslie. Use your head. He can't talk to you.

I took a deep breath in an attempt to calm myself.

"Justin," I said slowly and smoothly, "I know you can hear me. I know you're there, and I know you're scared. We're on the tap system, remember. You don't have to move, but please answer me. I need to know."

I took another deep breath.

"Do you hear him again?"

A pause.

Tap-tap. Yes.

I closed my eyes, squeezed them shut, as if willing a bad dream to go away.

"Is he coming up the stairs? Do you hear him coming up the stairs?"

No response.

I amended my question.

"Is he upstairs already, Justin? Is he out in the hallway?"

Tap-tap.

My mind's eye assumed command. I saw myself pressed against that frozen window, backed into it like prey caught in a corner, with the predator just around the bend. I heard the soft footsteps moving methodically up the hallway toward the guestroom—my room. That narrow crack in the door, that chasm of hall. I saw a man coming to halt, bending slightly to peer through that crack, his eyes as dark as soil. Looking in. Just looking. I was frozen, paralyzed from the neck down.

But you're in a church, Leslie. Justin is the one frozen against the window with the footsteps coming. Do something.

"Justin, you need to move—you need to move now! I know you're scared, but you have to. I'm right here, Justin, right here next to you. Tiptoe across the guestroom real quick, back into the bathroom, do you hear? Go back into the alley, Justin. Go back into the alley."

Something twinged deep inside me, somewhere dark. I had called this play, the trip through the alley—to the window, then the escape down the trellis. It had been *my* idea to get out from under the bed.

I gritted my teeth.

I tried to imagine sounds of a boy shuffling quietly across a carpeted floor, but I was only creating hopes out of phone fuzz, for that was all I heard.

"Are you there, Justin? Are you in the bathroom?"

Tap-tap.

He'd made it. He'd acted, and he'd made it. But that tap-tapping was so deceptive. So unfeeling. So nothing. It wasn't as simple and clear and easy as that. There was no confidence or determination through that dismal piece of Morse code—just a naked answer.

He was glued to a wall, kneeling perhaps, tucked between the toilet and cabinet. Or lying face-down in the bathtub with the drape pulled. Panting ravenously. Sweating. Heart thundering in his small chest, his ears tuned to every possible sound.

"Can you still hear him, Justin?"

Tap-tap.

"Where is he? Oh, sorry, don't answer that."

I breathed deep.

"Is he in the hallway still?"

A pause. I waited.

Tap-tap-tap.

Three taps. Was there a mistake of some sort? I never imagined a seven-year-old could be so intelligent as to designate a new signal—not just without benefit of verbal communication but by the mere assumption that I would understand. I know better these days.

"Is that a maybe, Justin? Does three taps mean you aren't sure?"

Tap-tap.

"Can you hear him now?"

Before he could respond, I swear I heard something. It was low but audible, lost in the snowy static. Something in the background, semidistant. Think of all the noises you hear when you're on the phone with someone, the noises in that person's home, other people talking.

It sounded like a door creaking open.

"I heard that," I said. "Was that the guestroom door, Justin? Is he in the guestroom now?"

Eternity flew past.

Tap-tap.

I imagined the intruder entering the bathroom, moving the shower drape aside, finding Justin cowering in the corner, tears streaking down his cheeks, shivering. Hugging himself.

Get him out of there. Get him out now.

"Justin, get out of the bathroom. Get out of there quick before he gets all the way in the guestroom. Go back into your parents' bedroom. Get back under the bed, but be quiet. *Go.*"

The words poured off my lips like quicksilver. They were smooth and soft yet urgent. Not only did Justin move, he did so in sync with my command. I can't say I heard it, though maybe I did. I probably heard something, but he went on cue with my request. It was as if his body was obeying the commands of my mind.

I saw Justin's house through the Cyclopean eye in my head once again—that eye was rapidly acquiring instincts of its own. I saw Justin pattering back through the alley, across the bedroom carpet—as the intruder moved through the doorway, into the dark guestroom—dropping silently to his belly, rolling beneath the sanction of the king-sized bed again. Back where he had started from. In that uncanny perceptual manner I'll never be able to explain, I knew the answer to my question before I asked it.

"Did you do it, Justin? Are you under the bed again?"

Tap-tap.

"Good. Very good. You're a tough kid, Justin. You're handling this extremely well for someone your age. You're being very brave."

It was perhaps the most honest thing I'd said all night.

"Don't speak, Justin. We're staying on the tap system for now. So, he's in the guestroom still, right?"

Tap-tap. The taps rang through with an added measure of strength, perhaps to express the renewed security of being beneath the bed again … or maybe that was me, creating my own interpretations.

"Justin, I want you to stay where you are. Don't move from under the bed."

I wouldn't worry about that. Justin isn't going anywhere.

"Remember, he doesn't know you're in the house." I wondered what the perp might do next. Investigate the guestroom. Migrate to the master bedroom. Would he come through the alley?

And how about the red light on the phone housing? Will the intruder see that? Will he realize he's not alone in the house?

The first attempt foiled, I decided staying put was our best option. I was nervous, though, really nervous. I felt the dampness under my arms, the film of perspiration on my forehead. Mary was smiling in that what-a-great-day way of hers across the desk as she babbled into her phone, absorbed in whatever world hummed at the end of her line. I barely noticed, mired in the quags of my own.

That window. Freedom opposite a pane of glass, winter wind whipping past. But Justin could have been killed. The boy could have died following my orders.

I drew a deep breath. Exhaled.

I lifted my car phone to desk level and made a second attempt to dial the authorities. I put the car phone to my free ear, waiting. Again, it rang. Again I was greeted by a robotic female voice: "All lines are currently busy. Please try—"

"Dammit!" I hissed, hitting the End button on my private phone. Oh, there was going to be hell to pay for this when all was said and done. Storm or no storm, a communications breakdown of this magnitude was intolerable. The local dispatchers' office would be hearing from my attorney once the dust had settled.

Get a grip, Leslie. You don't have an attorney. And there's still the boy to worry about. Try the cops again later.

I reached for plan B like a blind man groping for balance in an unfamiliar room. All hopes considered, the perp would find what he wanted and leave. I thought about that red light on the phone unit but restrained myself from asking Justin if there really was one. I figured there probably was, but that it wouldn't help to have him brooding over it also.

I asked him questions to which he tapped back the answers. Small stuff mostly, to keep his mind engaged. We talked and tapped for several minutes before I stopped in midsentence, wondering if this was a mistake.

Could the intruder hear me? If he comes through the alley and into the bedroom, will he hear my voice coming through the phone? From under the bed?

"One thing, Justin. As a precautionary measure. He's not in the bedroom with you now, is he?"

Tap.

"If you hear him come in, I want you to breathe into the phone. Breathe heavily and slowly. Then I'll know to stop talking. He probably couldn't hear me, but I want to be careful. All right?"

Tap-tap.

Then, from nowhere, a new thought hit me.

"Justin, how did you know about us? I mean, well, you knew the eight-hundred number." I paused before asking, "Have you called us before?"

I was greeted with silence, peppered with a snowy static. Silence has a sound: the sound of waves crashing against the seashore; wind rustling the forest canopy; automobiles speeding west on a six-lane highway. A kid shifting, propped on his elbows, mentally debating something that perhaps not even he understands. A question followed by a silence so chock full of other questions.

I didn't repeat the question. People on the other end of the line have a way of thinking that lets you know they're thinking. Calculating an answer, wondering if there's a correct response. We call that loud thought. When you've been at it long enough—a year and a half for me—loud thought becomes eerily recognizable.

Tap-tap.

"Have you talked to me before?" I couldn't recall ever having spoken with him.

Tap.

"Have you called us more than once?"

Tap-tap.

"During the afternoons mostly?"

Tap-tap.

"Your parents aren't home during the day, are they?"

Tap.

"Must be lonely, huh?"

Tap-tap.

"Is that why you call usually? Loneliness? Boredom?"

A hesitation. Loud thought. My Lotensin blipped over to 8:09 p.m.

Tap-tap-tap.

That response led to some hesitation of my own, some loud thought on *my* end of the line. I ran my tongue along my top row of teeth. All I could do was wonder.

"You sound confused, Justin. Is there something you're unsure of? Something you'd like to talk about, maybe?"

No response. Loud thought. I began to represent the absence of a response as an indication of uncertainty. I saw him gnawing his bottom lip, as if chewing on a thought that didn't quite know how to come out.

"Things are complicated, aren't they?"

Tap-tap.

"Hard to talk about, right? Hard to find the right words for."

Tap-tap.

"It's okay to feel confused," I told him. "A lot of kids grow up feeling unsure about things. Myself included. As a child, whenever I was confused about something, I'd go sit on the edge of an old train bridge not far from my house. I'd watch the trains go by underneath. I used to let my legs dangle over the edge of the concrete. I would sit there until it got dark out. I remember one night when my friend Becky and I were sitting up there after dinner, watching trains go by and talking. We were twelve or thirteen. Not much older than you."

I paused, thinking for a moment, before continuing. "Anyway, Becky's sandal slid off her foot as we were getting up to leave. We watched it fall all the way down. It landed in the middle of the train tracks. We couldn't get down either of the banks to get it because the prickers were too thick on both sides, so Becky had to skip home on one foot, sort of. I helped her, though. It wasn't that far. But I never went back to sit on that bridge again. Seeing that sandal fall all the way to the bottom made me too scared to go back."

I was perplexed at the turn the conversation was taking, but I did nothing to obstruct its course.

"You okay, kid?"

Tap-tap.

"Good. Just remember you can call us anytime, as often as you like. Okay?"

Tap-tap.

"How's everything going over there? Hear anything?"

Tap-tap.

"What—no, sorry, don't answer that." I bit down on my lip, searching for a way to ask the question in yes or no form. "Is he in the guestroom still?"

Tap.

"He's not?"

Tap.

"He's not in the guestroom anymore?"

Tap!

I hesitated. "Is he in the master bedroom?"

"Just went down the hall, to the study," the boy whispered. His words were barely decipherable through the phone static.

I didn't question his decision to speak. He was the better judge of that than I.

"He's in the study now?"

"Yeah."

"And the study is at the end of the hall?"

"Uh-huh."

"Did you see this person's face? When he came out of the guestroom, maybe?"

"No, just his feet. He's wearing boots."

"Okay, stay calm and stay put, Justin. You'll be fine. When he comes into the bedroom, don't make a sound."

"He's gonna come in here?"

Oh, yes. You bet he is. Do we tell Justin the truth and worry him now? Or wait until it happens and then deal with it?

"It's a good bet he will, Justin, and I'll tell you why. To be honest, I don't understand why he didn't go in there first. He's gonna come in and look for your mother's jewelry. Just keep quiet and let him do it. He'll hopefully leave the house after he finds what he's looking for."

"But it's all in her wooden chest," he replied in a tremulous whisper.

"Well, that's good, actually," I told him, "because then he won't have to go hunting around for it."

"But she keeps her chest right here under the bed."

I fell silent for a moment, gathering that one in.

"The chest is under the bed?"

"Uh-huh."

"Under the bed with you?"

"Uh-huh."

"Can you see it?"

"Yeah, it's right behind me, by my foot." His voice was wavering, with higher and higher fluctuations.

Watch your voice. You're unsettling him. Calm down, Leslie, calm down.

I smoothed it out.

"Okay, just sit tight for a minute while I think, Justin."

"Is he gonna find me?"

"No one is going to find you," I told him.

"He's gonna look under here, though."

"Justin, settle down—"

"But the box is under here, he's gonna find me—"

"Justin, you must relax. You're raising your—"

"I'm scared, Leslie, I'm really—"

"Justin, be quiet!" Silence fell between us for a moment—me listening to my breath, him to his thundering heartbeat. A part of me feared he'd start crying. He couldn't afford to lose his composure now, with the intruder this close.

"Just breathe, Justin, okay? Don't say anything. Relax for a minute. I'm going to relax also because I'm as scared as you are right now, and that's the honest truth."

"He's gonna look under here, isn't he?"

You can't keep him there, Leslie. No way. The perp will look under the bed. After he hunts around long enough, he'll get down on his hands and knees for a quick peek. He'll find the jewelry box, but he'll find Justin also.

"We're gonna need to get you out of there, Justin, so listen up. He's still in the study, right?"

"Yeah," he said, quavering.

"Relax, Justin, everything's going to be okay," I told him, though I had no way of knowing that for sure. "I want you to slide out from under the bed, *to your left.* Is that clear? Slide out on your left side. And do it quietly."

"Right now?"

"Right now."

"What if he comes out?"

Yeah, Les, what if the intruder comes out? What then? Justin's the one in there, not you.

I cursed myself for failing to foresee this predicament. I had backed us into a corner, and now we had to walk on wet paint to escape.

"You're not going to do anything yet. Just do what I tell you. Go back to tap talking, first of all. I don't want him to hear anything."

"Okay. What next?"

"Don't talk. We're tapping now, right?"

Tap-tap.

"Roll out to the left."

Tap-tap.

"You did already?"

Tap-tap.

"Everything okay?"

Tap-tap.

"Good. Just stay calm, and you'll be fine. I'm right here with you. I want you to tiptoe to the left-hand edge of the main door, the one that goes out to the hallway. But don't *cross* the doorway, don't show yourself. Just go to the edge of it."

A pause.

Tap-tap.

"Everything clear?"

Tap-tap.

"Can you peek down the hallway, down to the end?"

Tap-tap.

"All clear?"

Tap-tap.

The perp was still in the study.

This was the moment of truth. I hoped to God the study was stacked plentiful with interesting and valuable artifacts. A few seconds were all I needed. A precious, so critical few.

"First room on the left is yours, right?"

Tap-tap.

"Can you make it, Justin? Think you can make it?"

Tap-tap-tap.

"Are you willing to try?"

Tap-tap-tap.

The kid was terrified, but I had to push him here. I had no alternative.

What about the guestroom? The perp's already been through the guestroom, so chances are he won't revisit it.

*Have the boy hide out in there, under the bed or something.
Wait it out. This is too dangerous.*

Five minutes ago, that might have seemed a plausible
course of action, but not now, not this close—this close to the
escape. Now there was no turning back. We were paces away
from getting out. First room on the left. Down the spiral
stairs. Out the front door. To a neighbor's house. Freedom.
Safety.

I didn't dare pause to consider the implications of Justin's
vulnerability. For those few, precious seconds the boy would
be exposed. If the perp just happened, by coincidence, to step
into the hall as the boy broke for his room—

"Now, Justin, now! Go, go! Now!"

A quick, sharp breath—then nothing. I held my breath
and waited. It wasn't until I felt the immediate tension in my
chest that I realized Justin had done the same thing—sucked
in a hard breath and then held it.

The Cyclopean eye opened wide in my mind. I saw Justin
tucking his head down, refusing to look beyond his bedroom
doorway—were the intruder to emerge from the study, Justin
would rather not know it. Instead, his eyes were fixated on
the door to his bedroom. It was close and getting closer. It
was four feet away. It was two feet away. I heard Justin's bare
feet snicking across the hall carpet. And then …

"Are you there, Justin? Are you in your bedroom?"

Tap-tap.

He'd made it. Thank God. I let the air out of my chest.
My pulse still throbbed in my neck, but I saw everything
clearly now. Justin's escape route stood before him. He was
virtually free. All he had left to do was go down the spiral
stairs and out the front door.

"Be quiet going down the stairs, Justin. We're not home
free yet. Walk slowly and softly."

Tap-tap.

I waited several moments and then asked, "Okay, so we're in the downstairs den now, right?"

I waited.

No response.

Waited. Waited.

Nothing.

"We're in the den, right? Justin?"

No response.

"Justin?"

I waited, waited some more. Silence.

"Justin, are you there?"

Silence has a sound. The sound of buzzards soaring an aqua sky, riding hot coils of air in search of food. The empty whoosh of a person falling, down and down, legs and arms wheeling ... a pregnant void just prior to impact. The moment of stillness after lighting a cherry bomb on the Fourth of July and then running to get away from it ... waiting, waiting—*boom!*

My Cyclopean eye saw Justin standing partway down the spiral stairs.

"Justin, what's going on? Are you in the den yet?"

"He came downstairs," he whispered, barely audible.

Impossible.

"What? You hear him?"

"Other side. Kitchen, dining room ... he's somewhere over there."

"Justin, get off the stairs. Get off there and get behind something, a couch or a chair or something. Just get off the stairs."

Silence as he moved.

What the hell is going on here? The intruder was in the study, wasn't he? How could he have gone back downstairs so quickly? And what about the jewelry? He hasn't even visited the master bedroom yet.

Unless ...

CHAPTER 5

I CURSED MYSELF AGAIN on my lack of foresight and spun a full circle on my foam-padded swivel chair. It squeaked in that high-tone, rustic squeal that ancient furniture is known for. We'd like to petition for an upgrade in furnishings as much as phone lines, but to whom? As far as anyone here was concerned, redecorating was a pipe dream, even in a community as affluent as Sheldon.

Get behind something, Justin. Don't stand there frozen on the stairs like that.

Until now, the inkling that there may be more than one intruder in Justin's house had eluded me. Why hadn't I considered this possibility earlier? What had I been thinking?

Never mind that now, Leslie. You're doing the best you can. What's done is done. You and Justin are downstairs now. You're in the den. Move on.

"Where are you, Justin? Don't answer me if he's too close."

I was greeted by silence. Boy, did it have a sound. I was beginning to search my brain for a yes-no when he responded verbally.

"Okay," he said.

"Are you safe?"

"I think. I'm behind the sofa, in the back."

"In the back? The back of the den, you mean?"

"Yeah. Can't see me here."

"What if he walks through? Can he see you then?"

"Only if he looks back here. He won't, will he?"

"Is the couch against the wall, Justin? Is that what you're telling me?"

"Uh-huh."

"So, you're behind the couch, which is up against the back wall of the den, correct?"

"Yeah. I had to squeeze back here, so I couldn't talk for a minute."

"That's okay, Justin. That's perfectly fine. I'm glad you did what you did."

"He won't look here, will he?"

"No, he won't. As long as you keep quiet, he won't look back there. Just hold still and keep your voice low. Go back to tap if he comes near."

"I hear him now," he whispered.

"Where is he?"

"Mom's good room, I think. I'm not allowed to go in there. All her good stuff's in there."

"What kind of good stuff?"

"White plates and cups."

China. Expensive glassware. Probably an ivory-white carpet, virgin of a shoe sole.

"He's opening the doors where Mom's white plates are. I got punished for doing that."

"Well, don't worry about him, Justin. Just stay where you are, and you'll be fine."

"How'd he get down here like that? The steps go down to the living room."

"Where is the living room, Justin?"

"Over by the garage, past the kitchen."

"You're saying the living room is on the other side of the house?"

"Uh-huh."

"I think there may be more than one person in your house, Justin. I think the first man is still upstairs. He might be in your mom and dad's room right now, so what you did was good."

"Someone else?"

"That would be my guess right now, but you shouldn't get too scared about it. You're safe behind that couch. Just stay put and tell me if anything happens." As an afterthought, I added, "You're sure your parents didn't tell you when they were coming back?"

"No. Just went out."

Where could they be? In a snowstorm like this, where on earth would a married couple go?

One thing was clear. Justin's parents had attended some sort of planned event. There were two reasons supporting this. First, a couple didn't decide spur-of-the-moment to go out for dinner on a night predicted to be the recipient of half a foot of snow. They'd had an engagement—an office party or organizational meeting, perhaps. Second, a pair of thieves with any semblance of intelligence didn't draw up a scheme to rob a house in the middle of a snowstorm when, one would be inclined to suspect, everyone would be indoors for the night. The home invasion had been planned well in advance, meaning the perpetrators had known of the engagement Justin's parents had meant to attend. The one thing they hadn't counted on was a seven-year-old boy being left alone in the house.

There were now two intruders to account for. Could there be others? I wondered what our chances were of reaching the front door if the second perp migrated to the top floor also. Did Justin have a clear path in which to run? Could he get out and safely reach a neighbor's house?

"Justin, tell me something. What is the closest door to you now?"

"Uh, the front one. Across from the kitchen."

"If you were standing in the kitchen, could you see the front door?"

"Uh, yeah. There's a short hallway, kind of."

"What other doors are there?"

"The one that goes out to the garage—"

"From the living room, right?"

"Yeah."

"Which is on the other side of the house?"

"Uh-huh, yeah."

Too far. Too risky.

"Any others?"

"Back door. The sliding one that goes out to the deck."

"What room is that one in?"

"Living room."

Both in the living room. Both too far.

"Is that it?"

"Yeah."

"How close are you to the front door, Justin?"

"It's right next to the den. But it's got too many locks."

Too many locks?

"So, it's right next to the room you're in—that's what you're saying?"

"Yeah, but it's locked a lot."

"If the other man went upstairs also, do you think you could make it out the front door, Justin?"

"No, it's too scary. It's got locks."

I knew exactly what he meant. The front door, the main door of the house, was battened down. It had a standard knob lock, deadbolt latch, and chain lock—the works. Think through the eyes of a seven-year-old. Three locks on that door: three simple devices, three simple procedures. But now insert the variables. There are strangers in your home, prowling about like phantoms. Suddenly, those three simple procedures become one complex, terrible task. Remove the chain, flip the deadbolt, twist the knob lock, pull the door open, and then open the storm door—all at once. Shaky hands. Sweaty fingers. Someone behind you. All that noise. Someone would hear. You could probably make it, but was it worth trying? Was it worth the terror?

I decided not to move him. It was his house and his life. Likewise, it would be his hands doing the jitter trying to undo those locks, not mine. The crawlspace behind the couch seemed like a suitable hideout. If he wanted to stay put and wait it out, then so be it. I was with him.

I could only wonder when his parents might return. If the crooks finished their job and left the house, Justin would surely insist that I remain on the phone with him until Mom and Dad arrived. I would gladly comply. The thought of an eerie silence in a house that's just been robbed and possibly ransacked was enough to raise the hairs on the back of my neck. That silence would have a deafening sound. Justin, I knew, would refuse to move. The narrow space behind the sofa would be his hideout until his parents walked through the door. Even then, he might cower in doubt, awaiting the sounds of his parents' voices before crawling out. I thought about that cordless phone also. How much longer would it last?

"All right, Justin, this is what we're gonna do. It seems like you're in a pretty safe spot, so we're gonna hang tight for a while and see what happens. In the meantime, I want you to go back to tap-talking. It's best if you're as quiet as possible. Remember, we have to pretend that you're not there, right?"

"Uh-huh," he whispered.

"Okay, no more talking until I tell you. Remember, one for no, two for yes, three for not sure. Got it?"

Tap-tap.

I took a moment to delve into my mind for something to talk about. Try to recall the last time you were asked to devise a one-sided conversation over the phone. I suppose we could have shared the silence, but such an approach didn't seem conducive to keeping Justin immersed in the semirelaxed state in which I wanted him, where he was safer and less prone to panic. Thus, I racked my brain for something interesting to say, something that involved the boy himself, and that included tappable responses. Focusing on the questions I asked would help soften his anxiety.

Across the desk joint, Mary was engaged in a conversation of her own. I spared her a quick glance and saw her smiling face with the phone tucked between her cheek and shoulder, reading aloud from her manual of ribrackers. Mary had a richness in her voice that seemed to epitomize her natural elegance for this kind of work.

Between calls of my own, I would often tune in to her. Not to the words themselves but to her mitigating timbre, so smooth and soft. It was almost maternal. I couldn't help but conjure up warm memories of my own mother—sitting on her lap late at night, her delicate voice floating past my shoulders as she read from *Mother Goose*, the book sprawled before us like a sacred world. Occasionally, Dad would join us, and I'd nestle between them, but it was my mother who always read. It was her voice that transported us from our world to another, made us together, and lulled me into a warm slumber on those special nights. When you're a kid, it's often the present you think about. Sometimes the past, rarely the future. The harsh realities of life haven't revealed themselves, not solely because of your age but because your parents have been there to shield you with their protective wings. As an only child, that's what I most remember about those moments, when I was cuddled between them—feeling warm, loved, and protected. My parents were the best friends I ever had.

*   *   *

"Nine-one-one, what is your emergency?" a terse male voice answered.

I said, "Are you aware this line has been busy? I've been trying to get through for the last twenty minutes."

"We're swamped here, ma'am. The storm has lines down in three locations. There are a ton of accidents."

"Listen, I've got a serious situation here. I'm calling from the latchkey helpline on Main and Fifth. I have a boy on the line who says his house has been broken into. He's home alone, and we think there are two intruders in the house with him. You're gonna need to get someone out there."

"What's the address?"

"He's only seven. He either doesn't know his address or he can't recall it at the present time. I was hoping you could trace—"

"You don't have an address? Lady, I really can't afford to spare any units on another false alarm from you people. Not on a night like this."

"This is *not* a false alarm."

"Do you have any proof that this boy is telling the truth?"

"Are you kidding? He's terrified. If that isn't proof enough—"

"Call me back in ten minutes, okay? If he still insists the story is true, we'll try and get somebody out."

My car phone went dead.

*   *   *

"Sounds to me as if you're alone a lot. Am I right about that, Justin?"

Tap-tap.

"Hmm," I said. "Must get lonely there by yourself, huh?"

Tap-tap.

"Not much to do."

No response.

"Loneliness can be a difficult thing to deal with. Oftentimes it seems so quiet you start to think the walls are staring at you. When I went away to college, I was faced with loneliness too—kind of like yours, only I was a bit older. My roommate dropped out of school. She never told me why, really. Anyway, I had to live by myself for the rest of the school year, and it wasn't easy for me. I didn't have a phone in my dorm room, and I didn't know many people at the school. There were times I swear I would have done anything to have someone to talk to. Sometimes it's nice just to be able to talk to another person. Not so much to hear what they're saying but for the sake of being with someone. You know what I mean, Justin?"

Tap-tap.

"You know, I think you'd really like having a dog. A dog is great to have around because, in a way, he's always there for you. A dog will never get mad or get in a bad mood or get grumpy. He always wags his tail and is happy to see you. You can pet him, and he'll wag his tail and ask for more. I had a real nice dog when I was a kid, and I've been thinking about getting one for my own little boy."

Tap.

"What? You think I shouldn't get a dog?"

No response. I waited a minute. Perhaps the absence of a response was a signal that I had asked the wrong question.

"Is it that you don't like dogs, Justin?"

Tap.

"You *do* like dogs?"

Tap-tap.

I pondered a moment longer, chewing on my bottom lip.

"Is it that your parents won't let you have a dog? Wait, let me rephrase that. *Will* your parents let you have a dog?"

Tap.

"They won't let you?"

Tap.

"Have you asked them?"

Tap-tap.

"Oh, that's too bad. Dogs are nice to have." The thought of that boy and his dog, Mickey, playing together after school each day reentered my mind. "Was it your mom who said no, Justin?"

Tap.

"Your dad?"

Tap-tap.

"Well, I guess we can't have everything, can we?" I leaned back in my swivel chair—*creak!*—and switched ears with the receiver. My earlobe had developed a dull soreness from having the hard plastic pressed up to it. The boy's mentioning of his parents had opened an inner door for me, and I couldn't help but speculate. Despite the little I'd learned so far, things in Justin's home did seem a little off center. Though he hadn't expressed any clear examples of troubles in his family, the clauses of doubt and hesitation he'd employed in his responses had raised some red flags in my mind. I didn't know what those flags signified, or if they meant anything at all. Much of the Call-A-Friend service is guesswork and assumptions, and I was well aware of the perils of guessing too far and assuming too much. Then again, children of healthy families have little reason to dial 1-800-FRIENDS, do they?

Unfortunately, the well-balanced family is growing far and few between. Statistics indicate a 96 percent dysfunction rate in today's world. With figures like those, it's little wonder help lines like ours are spreading throughout the country. In the nineties, kids have plenty to be confused about. One of every ten people will become alcoholic. That's close to one alcoholic for every two families. One of every two couples will divorce. Kids who develop without the benefit of a father or mother figure face distinct disadvantages compared to those who have both. One of every three girls will be sexually, physically, or emotionally abused. And in today's economy, more and more families involve two working parents, whose children are sometimes left home alone. They are the latchkey kids of our society.

Justin seemed a prime example. I harbored little doubt to there being some measure of unhappiness in his home. The only question was his willingness to discuss it—often a Herculean task for children. Kids will tip off their loneliness and inherent unhappiness but often clam up when it comes to pinpointing the actual problem. Many will avoid the issue and provide evasive answers to direct questions. I have a theory that many are torn between an unconscious love and hate for their parents—love for the parental figure, hate for the parental problem. The majority of conflicts that parents endure are beyond the child's scope of comprehension, which often complicates matters. Some will use denial as their way of coping. If they pretend it's not there, it won't be. The worst of experiences are sometimes repressed, when an often horrific event is relocated to the subconscious mind and actively forgotten. A spectacular process such as this can lead to many problems later in life.

Tina Lehman is my best example of the latter case. We went to college together, though we never knew each other or as much as exchanged hellos. What I do know is that Tina was a senior when I was a junior, and that she freaked out right around the time I started dating Richard. She'd been watching a movie with her roommate one night, in which a male character subtly coerced a younger woman into having consensual intercourse. Midway through the scene, the Lehman girl began to scream. The screams escalated into a fit of rage and horror that left the roommate both perplexed and terrified. Arms thrashing, eyes blazing, Tina Lehman began to pull her own hair out. Then she tried to scratch her eyes out. Then she ran out of the room and burst into the dormitory hallway, where she proceeded to bang her head into the painted cinderblock wall with suicidal force. She gave herself a concussion and wound up in a psychiatric ward. She was twenty-one years old. I later learned that Tina had been forcibly raped at age eleven by a dishwasher repair man. For a full decade, Tina had no knowledge she'd been assaulted because she'd repressed the event immediately after it'd happened. Ten years later, the memory had resurfaced, without warning, as she had watched a similar event parlayed in a movie. The attacker was tracked down, convicted, and sentenced to jail time.

I had no reason to believe any such demon resided within the walls of Justin's home. But the scales were slightly out of tune. If the two of us were going to be on the phone a good while longer, perhaps I could find out why.

"Well, Justin, I was thinking we could talk a little more about your situation at home. I know you expressed some confusion earlier, and I'm willing to talk about it if you are. Do you feel comfortable with that?"

A pause. Loud thought.

Tap-tap.

"All right," I began. "How about your parents? Do you mind if I ask you some questions about your parents?"

I made sure to speak slowly and smoothly. I knew I was addressing a delicate subject. I molded my questions carefully, aiming to progressively increase Justin's confidence in speaking candidly. Of course, I'd be the one speaking. He'd be tapping.

I waited a moment before the reply came through.

Tap.

No, he didn't mind. Good start.

"You don't mind?" I repeated, to convey my respect for his privacy.

Tap.

"Okay, but if I start to move into things that you don't wish to talk about, make sure you let me know, all right?"

Tap-tap.

I nibbled the top of my fingernail clean off my right pinkie, searching for an adequate place to begin. I didn't want to leap into the heart of the matter right away, fearing it might dissuade him from further discussion. Moving into delicate matters is a slow process. As a stranger, perhaps it wasn't my place to delve into such personal concerns ... but I *was* anonymous, and this *was* an out-of-the-ordinary call-in. As far as I saw it, this was my job. More importantly, Justin's mind needed to be diverted from the dangerous men lurking inside his house.

"Being seven years old, you may be unsure how to answer this question, but I'll ask it anyway. You are an only child, you said, right?"

Tap-tap.

"Would you say that your mom and dad get along well together? At least when you see them?"

I waited patiently for a response. The loud thought that greeted me signified the boy's uncertainty.

Tap-tap, finally.

"They *do* get along okay?"

Tap-tap.

I was about to ask the question in a different way when a new response came through.

Tap-tap-tap.

He wasn't sure. I was positive it was an amendment to his previous answer, and a sure signal that there *was* some unrest between his parents. Often, instead of nodding or saying yes to a personal question, kids will shrug or murmur or look down, indicating confusion or outright avoidance.

"You're not sure how your parents get along, Justin?"

Tap.

"Do you ever see or hear them fighting with one another?"

No response. I waited.

"Do they fight sometimes?"

Tap-tap.

"Do they fight a lot?"

Tap.

"So, just sometimes then."

Tap-tap.

"Does it frighten you a little to hear them arguing about something?"

Tap-tap.

"Well, that's perfectly understandable. No child enjoys hearing his parents fight with one another. But all parents have their disagreements. In fact, my mom and dad were two of the best people I've ever known, and even they had their share of heart-to-heart squabbles."

Where are they? I wondered, thinking of Justin's parents. My Lotensin read 8:23 p.m. The snow drifts would be piling up by now, and we usually closed the office by nine thirty. Then there was the babysitter to worry about …

"How 'bout you, Justin? Do you get along with your parents all right?"

It was a sticky question, but I was running short on things to say. It's one thing to have to pilot conversations over the phone with strangers, but something else to have to pilot a *one-sided* conversation.

Tap-tap.

"Well, that's good," I said with reassurance. "I thought you did."

I probed my thoughts for more possibilities, questions of a general nature that might help narrow things down to what I was looking for. Given the subtleties of family chemistry and the inner conflicts that disrupt it, I was quickly realizing how difficult it might be diagnosing the problem on my own. The tap system denied Justin the freedom to express his thoughts verbally, leaving it up to me to figure it out. I also had to consider that it was likely he wouldn't speak his mind *regardless* of our system of dialogue—not unless he truly wanted to.

Perhaps you're overanalyzing things here, Leslie. Maybe he's just lonely, huh?

I decided to climb out on a limb.

"Justin, do either of your parents ever drink a lot? Like beer or booze? Stuff like that?"

He probably won't even know what that is at his age. He can't even—

Tap-tap.

I stiffened a bit, more by the authority of the response, I think, than the response itself.

"Is this both Mom and Dad we're talking about, Justin?"

Pause. Waiting.

Loud thought.

Tap.

"Is it your dad?"

Tap-tap.

"Do you see your father drinking often?"

Another hesitation. Phone static.

Tap-tap-tap.

"You probably see him at night, don't you? After work, maybe?"

Tap-tap.

"Does he usually drink every night, Justin? At least, that you can see?"

Tap-tap.

Which means he probably drinks more that the boy doesn't see.

I often wonder which is held in higher esteem in America today—family and home life, or the race to get ahead in professional life: the lust for money and status. There are workaholics who come home at night needing alcohol to quell their nerves. They're too bushed for the family, too drained to give anything more. A couple of drinks and off to bed. Up the next morning and back to work. You can call me a cynic, but I live in Sheldon and deal with children of these types three nights a week. I even married a workaholic, but he's been dead for four years now, going on five.

"Does your dad sometimes get mean when he drinks in your house, Justin?"

Tap-tap.

"Does he get mean a lot?"

Tap.

"Just sometimes?"

Tap-tap.

The question of physical abuse occurred to me, but I dismissed it. Somehow, through a weathered perception I can't explain, abuse didn't seem to fit the mold here.

"How about Mom? Does she drink very much?"

Tap.

"Just Dad?"

Tap-tap.

"Your dad works hard, doesn't he?"

Tap-tap.

"Tell me something, Justin. Do you and your parents ever get together and do things on weekends? Like bike riding or kite flying? A trip to the zoo maybe? Things like that?"

A spell of silence prompted me to amend the question. I felt I knew the answer.

"You don't do those things too often, do you?"

Tap.

"I didn't think so. How about friends, then? Any other boys your age in the neighborhood that you like to play with?"

Tap-tap-tap, came the response.

I was baffled.

"I'm not sure what you mean by that, Justin."

Tap-tap-tap.

"You're not sure if there are any boys in your neighborhood? Is that what you're saying?"

Tap-tap-tap.

Something was amiss here. I knew I had stumbled onto something, but I wasn't sure how to further proceed. My best guess, incorporating all I'd learned during the conversation, was the simple notion that Justin was a classic latchkey, and a very lonely one. Perhaps the boy had no friends. I remembered the other lad and his dog, Mickey, and something hurt inside me. My heart grew suddenly sore for this lonely and frightened boy of seven, squeezed into the crawlspace behind the den sofa while strangers moved through his home. I wanted to reach out and hug him through the phone line, provide him with the love my parents had bestowed upon me, put my mouth to his ear and tell him that things were going to be okay.

"Do you know of *any* boys in your neighborhood, Justin? Any at all?"

No response.

I waited patiently, wondering what was worth hiding with regard to the question. The vagueness of his responses lent some suspicion toward how much he was telling me. Or how much he *wasn't* telling me.

"Justin? Do you feel uncomfortable with this question?"

I waited some more.

"I won't ask if you are."

Silence. Static.

He wasn't answering.

"Would you prefer we drop the issue entirely?"

No response.

I waited. Ten seconds. Fifteen. Twenty.

"Justin? Can you hear me?"

No answer. Nothing.

Suddenly, my heart found the fast lane. Something wasn't right.

"Justin?" I asked, tension in my voice now. "Justin, is something wrong? Tell me what's wrong."

Nothing. Nothing at all.

What is happening here?

I raised my voice. "Justin, please answer me, tell me—"

Heavy static, like a hard wind or … *breathing.* Suddenly it hit me, and my fingers tightened around the receiver. The boy was breathing, breathing into the phone.

Someone was in the den with him. I remembered our cue from the master bedroom, and my muscles stiffened. Had the perp heard my voice coming through the phone from behind the couch?

I half-expected the boy to start screaming, but there was only the light seashore static of phone fuzz. For the first time tonight, I was scared, truly and deeply scared. Me, a twenty-eight-year-old woman in this creaking swivel chair in the Call-A-Friend regional base.

I kept the phone pressed to my ear, listening tensely, hoping my voice hadn't been detected. In all likelihood, Justin had one hand over the earpiece of the receiver to muffle my voice. Realizing this, I decided it was best to keep quiet and sit still. And wait.

Someone was in his den. Probing and poking around. A man whom I suddenly feared was extremely dangerous.

In a way, I felt helpless, holding a phone here in the church basement. All I could do was wait. My heart was pounding.

Silence on the other end.

Be with us now, I prayed, clenching a fist and gnawing a knuckle. *Let him be okay. Just let him be okay.*

I closed my eyes and waited. Silence has a sound.

CHAPTER 6

I MET RICHARD IN the heart of my junior year. I was out on the campus green with some friends, eating an ice cream when he walked up to me. It was his fearlessness, I think, that most resonated with me. Most guys can't summon the courage to approach a girl in the presence of others and ask her out.

Richard did just that. I had never seen him before.

I was licking off the top of my cone when he approached from behind and tapped my shoulder. I turned around, and there he was: short brown hair, clean-shaven, a silk tie flapping against his chest. I looked him up and down, and vanilla ice cream dribbled across my lower lip. For a moment he said nothing. He stared at me, his lips gently set in a Mona Lisa smile.

He stuck his hand out. I shook it.

"My name's Rich. I transferred in last week, out of BU."

I was momentarily speechless. It takes the human mind several seconds to catch up when it's been caught off guard. I opened my mouth to reply, but he did that for me.

"You're Leslie, right?"

I nodded quizzically. "Yeah. Yeah, that's me. Nice to meet you."

My circle of friends had fallen silent. I felt their half-smiles around me.

Richard remained unflappable, his eyes unmoving. They were blue and deep.

"I was wondering if you'd like to go out sometime. Tonight maybe? Tomorrow? Some night this week."

His eyes remained planted on mine.

"You mean, like—"

"You know, just dinner. Nothing fancy. I heard the tavern up on the corner has good food."

That struck me also because the Red Bull Tavern had outstanding food. The guy had transferred in last week. Already he knew the restaurants and my name. What else did he know?

I felt the group power around me. The girls were tomb-silent as they watched and waited.

"Sure, I guess," I said, and he smiled confidently, as if he'd known from the start that I would oblige.

"Tonight okay?"

"Yeah, I guess. As good as any." I smiled genuinely, wondering what I was getting myself into.

"All right then. I'll meet you at … seven thirty?"

I nodded.

"Right here. We can walk."

"Great."

"I'll be looking forward to it," he said with that Mona Lisa look. Then he turned and ambled across the green, hands in his pockets. We watched him the entire way, but he never looked back.

For a minute, no one spoke.

"Well, *that* was strange," Ali mumbled from behind. I barely acknowledged her, transfixed by the back of Richard's button-down, growing smaller and smaller.

"Strange?" someone else said. "That was *easy*. It's not supposed to be that easy, Leslie."

Those words stuck with me. I agreed that it wasn't supposed to be that easy. My mother had warned me to be wary of aggressive men.

"Vultures, Leslie—that's what they are," she said. "They'll take advantage of you and then fly off in search of fresh meat."

But Richard turned out to be anything but a vulture. On the contrary, he was the most sincere man I'd ever met. I learned that evening that the aura of confidence he'd exuded that afternoon was his true self. He had no problem transgressing beyond small talk into deeper issues. Furthermore, he spoke with a degree of insight and understanding I hadn't encountered in a guy before, as though he related in some way to every facet of my life.

He paid for dinner and escorted me back to my dorm. He didn't kiss me. Rather, he shook hands and thanked me.

"I had fun," he said, boring into me with those sure eyes of his. "I really did. I hope we can do this again in the near future."

"Me too." I paused and then added, "My number's in the directory. Give me a call sometime."

"I will," he said. I knew he meant it. It was funny, I thought. One evening with this guy, and I already knew him—knew him on a subconscious plane of mind that was too natural yet too abstract to define.

A week later, the Lehman girl freaked out, sending vibes across the campus. By that time, Richard and I were officially together. We dated steadily throughout the remainder of our college lives and got engaged in the spring term of senior year. We married upon graduation.

Richard was immediately accepted by a major engineering firm in Sheldon that his uncle owned. Strings, strings, and more strings. Given the circumstances, Richard was destined for corporate ascent. It took him a mere three years to climb the corporate rungs that would probably require upwards of a decade from an ordinary employee. He had attained the position of vice president of finance by the time of his death.

His disease began months earlier, however. Patrick was born when we were both twenty-two, in the first full year of our marriage. I had conceived on our honeymoon.

After Patrick's birth, Richard was on his way in the corporate world and directing more and more of his attention toward that area. I was on maternity leave from my accounting firm with full benefits, home with the baby and keeping the apartment in order. That was one of the most fulfilling times of my life, nursing Patrick on the rear balcony, reading westerns and listening to the birds chatter incessantly around me. I was a mother, rearing my own child. It felt great to be alive.

Six months later, we moved into the house that Patrick and I still occupy, in the pith of Sheldon affluence. Richard was making more than most forty year-olds, and there was much ground to be consumed, he told me. Life was upon us, he said, resting in the cups of our palms.

"We're gonna be rich, Leslie, hon. You know that, don't you?"

I nodded, smiling. "And we're gonna go on trips and cruises every other month—"

"—Alaska—"

"—and live in this big house—"

"—the Amazon—"

"—and provide everything Patrick needs—"

"—BMWs, Porsches—"

"—but we don't want to spoil him—"

"—Jacuzzi …"

I jumped on him and assaulted him with kisses. On the cheeks, the forehead, the nose, the lips. I pressed my mouth into his, licked his tongue with mine. I gripped his shoulders tighter, feeling his sudden erection against my navel. I grew suddenly hot. I began undoing his top buttons and licking his chest.

"Hold up, honey, hold up for a sec."

I worked my hands down his shirt, ignoring him.

"Yo, hold up. Time out." He was trying to back away.

I held onto him, determined to win him out, do it on the floor if I had to.

He straightened his arms and pushed me away. I stood there looking at him, thwarted.

"What?" I asked.

"I don't want to jump into that yet."

I smiled.

"I know, it's tough because you're so beautiful, but—"

I advanced, but he stopped me.

"Leslie, I'm serious," he said with a dry laugh. "Not now. I've got some paperwork I want to finish up in the study."

"Crab."

"Save it for me," he said, backing toward the hall. "Keep the bed warm. When I get in there, I'm gonna exhaust you."

"Oh, you think so?"

"I know it."

"What makes you think you can pass me up for a later date all of a sudden?" I asked, smiling, trying to look seductive.

"'Cause you're my wife. And I love you."

"Hah," I said and whisked back to the bedroom to watch some television.

I outlasted two sitcoms and the first half of a TV movie. I kept it good and warm under the sheets. But by the time Richard came to bed that night, I was long asleep.

*   *   *

I awoke at seven the next morning. Richard's side of the bed was empty. I found a brief note downstairs on the kitchen counter, scrawled on a napkin:

> *Early start today. Have to take care*
> *of a few things in the office. Talk to you at*
> *lunch. Back for dinner.*
>
> *L. R-*

I slid the napkin into the trash can and fixed myself a bowl of corn flakes. I ate in silence, acutely aware of the eerie quiet inside the house: the grandfather clock ticking softly in the adjacent room; the low, mitigating hum of the refrigerator. But it was another element of the silence I was aware of today, some new essence that seemed to underscore it. It was a dullness, a hollowness, although I'd have never confessed to it back then. I know now, however, that the quality of a silence can reflect the quality of the mind. Silence had a sound, even then.

I finished half of the corn flakes and dumped the rest down the sink. Then I went back upstairs to get Patrick. I peered over the crib railing with a smile. He was lying on his back, eyes open, looking up calmly, as if waiting for me to arrive. Few sights have given me greater satisfaction. It's one thing to see or hold a human infant, but to *rear* one is extraordinary. I reached down for him and brought him up against my chest, kissing him on the head. My mother told me once that no one will ever love you more than your mother, and now I understand what she meant.

Patrick rarely cried in the morning. I often found him staring at the ceiling, as if absorbed in a quiet spell of baby contemplation. He still sleeps like a baby today, five and a half years later.

I took him out on the back deck to nurse him. The backyard was so natural in the morning, so serene. When I leaned back in my full-length chair to nurse, I slipped gently into the transpiring scene around me, became a functioning element of it. The birds were busy at that hour and always a pleasure to watch. The more time I spent observing them, the more I noticed how much their actions contribute to their survival. Everything a bird does appears to serve some necessary function. Watching them often made me consider some of the things we humans do that mean little or nothing to the furtherance of our daily lives. Watching television, for instance. Eating when we're not hungry, smoking cigarettes.

I became particularly intrigued by a family of sparrows nesting in a holly bush along the right-hand side of the yard, near the fence. For several weeks, a single male, having staked out this territory, worked furiously to construct a nest and defend the area simultaneously. Once completed, he would perch himself on a branch a foot above the nest, chasing away other sparrows—males, presumably—that approached his holly bush. I also noticed that two sparrows would not nest within a certain distance of each other. Birds of different species didn't seem to care, however. That same spring, a family of robins nested in a low branch of a silver maple not far from the holly bush. Farther back, a mockingbird clan moved into the shrubbery. It amazes me how much one can learn by the mere act of observation.

On this particular morning, I focused my attention on the sparrows in the holly bush. The chicks were a week old, and the parents were busy gathering food for them. I watched intently as Patrick nursed from my breast. Because most holly bushes aren't too dense like other shrubs, I could easily see the nest from my vantage point. If I listened closely, I could even hear the chicks peeping away.

The parents' quest to feed their young was constant. One would return with an insect morsel, loiter briefly, and then fly off for more. Minutes later, the other would zoom in and land on the edge of the nest, relinquish its finds, and then fly off again. The cycle never ended.

But a sustained observation of the sparrows in the holly bush inspired in me deeper insights than just the redundancy of their tasks. I marveled at the simplicity and cooperation inherent in their lives. Nothing was complicated. Nothing was questioned, as far as I could tell. It was just *done.* And it was beautiful. I have come to the conclusion that few things are as fulfilling as sitting down and watching nature work. It's ironic how simple it is ... yet we never understand until we take the time to sit and watch. Until we allow ourselves to blend in.

Blending in was easy for me back then. Nursing Patrick seemed analogous to the sparrows' search for insects in the yard. For that part of the day, with Patrick in my arms, I truly belonged.

But my observation of the sparrows on this morning seemed to divert me elsewhere instead of inviting me into the scene. Change often begins in subtlety, as I know now. Only years later do I realize the meaning of that vague sense of alienation I felt that sultry spring morning on my back deck.

If I had to anoint a vertex in the scheme of things, a point where things began to feel wrong, it was then. Somehow, unlike mornings prior, I felt like a human being looking into the scene instead of *being* inside it, *being* a part of it. I felt locked out.

It's amazing how change creeps up on you. You can't look into a mirror and decide how much your hair has grown in the last hour. Only when it drapes over your eyes and obstructs your vision do you discover you aren't seeing clearly anymore.

*   *   *

As time passed, Richard's lunchtime calls thinned out.

It was a gradual process. He'd forget a day, call me the next few, and then forget again. Eventually he'd dwindled his average to three calls a week, on select days when he wasn't "snowed under in the office." I asked him about it several times in bed, but the answer was always uniform. He was moving up in the business world, and advancement required time, even if it meant sacrificing several calls per week. It was the price to be paid for success.

"Don't worry, babe," he said, staring quietly at the ceiling. "Someday we're gonna have everything. Then you'll be proud of me."

"What do you mean *then*?" I asked, sitting up in bed, looking down at him. "I'm proud of you now, Richard. Do I make it seem like I'm not proud of you?"

"No, of course not," he said. His upward stare was unwavering.

I never understood what he found so engrossing about the ceiling—it was as if he was conjuring some divine futuristic image of himself. That's where Richard was wrong. He was too dead-set on thinking ahead, dreaming about what was going to be while the present flew past, unnoticed. "Maybe that came out wrong," he said. "Maybe I don't know what I meant. I'm kind of tired."

He turned on his side, away from me. I laid my hand on his shoulder and caressed him. It had been a while since we'd made love.

"Not tonight, honey. Got a long day tomorrow. Early start."

I slumped down in bed and turned on my side, away from him. "What else is new?" I mumbled, hoping he would hear.

I'm not sure if he did or not, but he never answered.

* * *

Before long, Richard's early starts became a daily happening. I'd wake up at six, and he'd be gone. Our breakfasts on the back deck came to an end, leaving only Patrick and me. And the sparrows.

His lunchtime calls dropped to one or two a week. Coupled with this was a drastic fall in the quality of the calls. No more smiles, happy thoughts, warm feelings. As the months passed and Richard's workaholism worsened, I began to realize that I didn't want him phoning me during lunch anymore.

His calls were hurried. Often his voice was tense, as if someone was watching, grading his performance from a balcony high in his office. We began to convey less and less, and before long the entire endeavor had lost its meaning.

I often heard voices in the background, phones ringing, machines humming. On a number of occasions, he had to cut our conversation short to return some important business calls. Some days the messages would be stacked miles high on his desk, according to what he told me, from people who needed to be called back because they were depending on him. The routine lunchtime love call became a lost cause in its own time. I soon realized that Richard's efforts to continue the routine were pure farce. I could tell by the impatience in his voice that it had become a time-consuming annoyance for him, ill-conducive to the endpoint of what needed to be accomplished.

Soon after, his "early start" had joined hands with a "late finish." I'd have dinner ready at five thirty, and he'd walk in at six with his briefcase, claiming he had some work to finish. Six became six thirty, a quarter to seven … sometimes seven o'clock.

It reached the point where I'd stand with hands on hips, watching crossly as he strode tiredly into the kitchen.

"Sorry, hon, I really am. Snowed under today. You wouldn't believe it."

Following an awkward pause, I asked, "So, everything's going well, I take it?"

"Oh, it's incredible," he told me, as he so often did. "Moving up like light speed."

I am able to realize nowadays the role I played in Richard's neurosis. So often I refused to address the problem, to reveal my unhappiness over him being gone all the time. Instead I'd ask a meaningless question, one that buried the issue and intensified his inebriating fervor. But change happens slowly. Perhaps I was too young and naïve to step outside of myself and wholly understand the problem. I know better today.

By the time Richard was promoted in the finance department, our dinners—those he made it to, that is—had assumed a startling similarity to his midday checkup call, which had been whittled to once a week. He sat at one end of the table, me at the other, Patrick next to me. We spoke less and less, and the words we did exchange, usually spurred by a question of mine, conveyed little. Often, Richard would look down at his food the entire time, as though his spinach and roast duck and mashed potatoes were more engaging than I was—or his child, for that matter. I tried posing questions now and then, sparking some real conversation, but he replied bluntly, shrugging his shoulders or mumbling under his breath. When dinner was over, he'd come around the table, kiss me on the forehead, and retreat to his study.

"Again?" I asked one night, Patrick in my arms. "Wouldn't you rather lie next to me on the couch or cuddle with your son?"

An obscure look passed over his face, a look of uncertainty, of momentary confusion. It was subtle, but it was there. I recognized that the decision between work and his family troubled Richard in some deep mental abyss.

Then he caressed Patrick's head and looked at me fretfully. "You know I want to, honey, but I can't. Not tonight."

"Why not? We miss you around here. Don't we, Patsy-Watsy?" I said, tickling the child.

"You'll have to get by without me tonight. Always work to do. Gotta finish up on some things."

"Yeah, we know. We know what's more important to some people, don't we, little guy?" Patrick squirmed playfully in my arms.

"Tell you what, then. Next weekend—not this one coming, but the one after—we'll go to the beach."

My eyes lit up. "You think so?"

"I know so. You can put it on the calendar. Write it in pen."

"You're sure you won't be working that weekend, though."

In addition to weekdays, Richard had started putting hours in every other Saturday. He'd work eight in the morning until one o'clock.

"Not that day I won't. We'll get a sitter for Pat. It'll be just you and me. How's that?"

"But do I have to wait that long to spend some quality time with you, unlike most other wives in the world?"

He grinned merrily but didn't reply.

He resigned to his study on the second floor as I resigned to kitchen cleanup and then some television.

Two Fridays later, Richard called from work to say he'd be home late, that I was to eat without him.

"Ready for some sun and sand?" I asked.

"I can feel it right now, sweetheart. And you next to me. Don't wait up for me. I'll probably be here a while."

As it turned out, I was in bed and sound asleep when he walked in. It had to be past ten thirty, I later surmised. I'd packed a beach duffel with towels, sunglasses, and sunscreen and left it on the hope chest by the windows, ready for tomorrow. I'd also made a pair of Italian subs for us and some iced tea, waiting in the refrigerator.

But Richard never woke me the following morning to go to the beach. I awoke on my own around seven thirty, and he was gone. Nonplussed, I ran around the house calling his name, but he didn't respond. With a sudden soreness in my throat, I ran out to the driveway. His car was missing. I stood on wobbly legs for a minute, thinking he'd perhaps made a quick trip to a deli or mini-mart to grab a few essentials and goodies before waking me. But then another thought came to me. I dashed into his upstairs study to look.

His briefcase was gone. Richard had left for the office.

I remember standing in the open doorway of his study, staring at the floor near the side of his desk where his briefcase should have been, feeling the sudden swelling in my eyes. I entertained the possibility that he hadn't returned home last night, but his side of the bed had clearly been slept in.

It still makes no sense to me today how someone of Richard's age and intelligence could be so irresponsible. For God's sake, I'd mentioned it to him over the phone the previous afternoon! So I guess I'd be lying if I told you I wasn't heartbroken. For the first time, I consciously felt alone and detached.

I made no effort to call the office. No part of me wanted anything to do with that office today. I retrieved Patrick from his crib and went out to the back deck to watch the sparrows. The tears welled, and I cried freely, letting them roll smoothly down my face in the soft morning. Patrick squirmed in my arms, perusing the yard with his curious brown eyes. The sparrows chipped and chirped, doing their thing. Never had I felt so ostracized from a scene I had once slipped into like a bathrobe.

Thirty minutes later, the phone rang. I got up to answer it. It was Richard.

"Oh God, honey, I'm so sorry. Oh, Jesus, I just remembered now, can't believe I forgot this. I know you were looking forward—"

"Don't worry about it," I told him glumly. "It wasn't anything to get excited about anyway, just a trip to the beach."

"Yeah, but I promised you, didn't I? Christ, I can't believe I did this. Honestly, I woke up and just thought I was on for today—"

"You're on every day, Rich."

There was a quick pause in his gush of words. "Yeah, but I wasn't today, and, you know, I didn't even realize it when I got here. I just sat down and got going."

What I most remember about that call was Richard struggling to explain the idiocy of his mistake and how shameful he felt. Not once did he raise the notion of just coming home. Looking back, I don't think he was waiting for me to *tell* him that, either. I doubt the idea ever pierced the bruised membrane of his thought process. That's the scary thing. It never *occurred* to him to simply come home.

"Don't worry over it, Richard. Things are fine, really. I'm okay," I said flatly.

"But I'm sorry, Les, I really am. I don't know how to be more sorry. How can I make it up to you?"

"You don't have to make anything up to me," I told him softly, and gently laid the phone on the hook.

I stood there, trembling. It was the first time I'd ever hung up on my husband.

That's when things really started to get bad.

CHAPTER 7

IT WAS DAVID BLOCK'S voice that gripped and shook me, bringing me back to where I was. That wasn't what scared me, though. Block's gravelly, cobblestone voice—the voice of a grandfather—was unapt to scare anyone. What frightened me were the dual forms of Sam Evans and Patty Lunesta gathered below the speakers of the old Fischer. Sam and Patty were hanging on Block's every syllable. I did not like the looks on their faces—Sam's especially.

David Block was the evening deejay at WMTS 109.8— our local oldies station. A lifelong Connecticut native and a fixture on the FM dial, Block had apparently forsaken his favorite Rialtos singles in lieu of traffic and weather updates. Gone were the relaxed and often sultry subtextures with which he normally spoke. Now he spoke in a clipped, fast-paced narrative. Sam and Patty were hunched over against the metal filing cabinet atop which the old Fischer sat, attuned to every word. A shadow darkened Sam's face. Patty shook her head.

There had been a crash on Route 7. A Greyhound bus had been involved. Details were uncertain at this time, but it was known that at least three passengers were seriously injured. Lines were down in several locations, and scattered power outages were being reported. Households without fireplaces or wood-burning stoves were facing a no-heat situation on a night in which the outside air temperature was twenty-six degrees—eleven above if you factored in the windchill. Utility crews were being scrambled to the affected regions, but some of the roads leading to those areas were impassable. Two house fires were being reported—one on Traveler's Hollow Road, the other on Treasure Grove. Kerosene-heater mishaps were the suspected causes.

Block: "We're being told the system has stalled over our area, creating worse-than-expected conditions. Previous forecasts of snowfall amounts in the six-to-seven-inch range have been upgraded to ten-to-twelve. Dangerous windchills are on tap for the tristate area. You are asked to remain in your homes unless absolutely necessary. We have also received word"—static … crackle … more static—"without heat are urged to refrain from reporting those outages via telephone, as power crews are already currently assessing damaged areas, and resources are limited. Again—"

I reached for my car phone and began dialing my home number. Halfway through, I stopped … I pressed the End button. The urge to call Tammy was overwhelming, maddening, but I fought it off. If the power in my house went out, Tammy would call me herself. She sat for Patrick three nights a week, she knew my private number, and she knew the drill. She knew she could spend the night at my place if the roads got too bad. It wouldn't be the first time she'd spent the night in the spare bedroom.

I had to remain focused on the situation at hand. Justin was still on the phone with me, silent and terrified and curled in a ball behind a sofa somewhere in the state amid one whale of a storm. I squeezed my eyes shut, trying to force out David Block's rock-filled voice, trying to ignore the concerned look on Sam's face (Patty's phone had rung, and she'd since gone back to her desk to answer it), trying to squelch my anxiety over Patrick and Tammy.

And trying not to think about Richard. Trying not to think about what happened. At a time like this, how could my thoughts possibly stray toward my husband's misgivings? What cruel divining rod was leading my memory down that dark path?

You must focus, Leslie. Put the past and the future out of your mind. The present is of vital importance right now. Why and how this was the case I could not fully understand. But here's the truth: I was at a crossroads, and a god-awful important one. It had something to do with Justin, something to do with my beloved Patrick ... something to do with Richard. I sat in the crosshairs of it all, both wanting and not wanting to know why. All I'd ever really wanted was to have done the right thing. You do the best you can, I guess. You do the best you can. And sometimes you still fail. *You still hear the screams in the daylight ... as if she'll never hit bottom. As if she'll never die. As if the sadness will never go out of her eyes. As if—*

I dialed 911 on my car phone. It was time to put an end to this madness. As the line rang, I pressed my desktop phone against my chest to muffle the mouthpiece. I didn't want Justin to hear my exchange with the dispatcher.

A female voice this time: "Nine-one-one, what is your emergency?"

"This is the fourth time I've called! Do *not* hang up on me!"

"How can I assist you, ma'am?"

"I'm a volunteer at the latchkey helpline on Main and Fifth. I have a young boy on the line. He's home alone, and there are two intruders—I repeat, *two intruders*—in the house with him."

"Where are the boy's parents, ma'am?"

"He doesn't know. He's only seven."

"Do the parents carry a mobile phone at which they—"

"Oh Christ, lady, don't you think I would've thought of that?" My impatience was beginning to ebb out my ears. "Trust me—I've already covered this territory."

"Okay, give me the address."

"He either doesn't know his address or he's too scared to remember it. But he was able to provide his phone number. Can you make an acquisition?"

"What's the phone number, ma'am?"

"It's 724-8159. Area code 618."

I heard the click-clack of computer keys. Felt the bump-thump of my pulse in my neck. I was getting close now. We were getting so close …

"Okay, ma'am, it'll take several minutes to make an acquisition. I have a unit on standby. He'll proceed to the address the moment we have one."

"The house is sure to be locked," I added quickly. "The officer may be able to gain access through the basement. Otherwise, he'll have to force his way in. Make sure you tell him that."

"Yes, ma'am, I'll be sure to tell him."

"Thank you." I hit the End button on my car phone. I deposited the phone into my purse.

Into my desktop phone I spoke, "Justin? Justin, are you there? Answer me if you can, Justin, please."

At best I was hoping for a tap, so I was surprised when he replied verbally.

"Yeah. I'm okay, I think."

I swelled with relief at the sound of his voice. My Lotensin read 8:39 p.m. We'd been on the phone for nearly an hour.

"Okay, Justin, the police are on their way to your house now. It may take them a few minutes to get there because of the snow. But they're coming, okay? Do you understand what I'm telling you?"

"Yeah."

"Stay where you are until they get there. You're still in the den, I take it?"

"No." He sounded cramped and constricted. "I moved to the laundry room. I'm in the dryer now."

"The dryer? You're *inside* the dryer?"

"Yeah. The man went back to the other side of the house, so I came in and crawled in here."

I was hesitant, unsure how to react to Justin's new sanction. "Can you fit okay? Does it … hurt at all?"

"I think I'm okay," he said in a whispering tone. I sensed he was directing half of his attention toward me, the other half toward noises in his home.

"Is the door open?" I asked. "The dryer door, I mean?"

"Just a little," he said. "So I can hear if anyone comes close."

"You know to use tap if anyone does, right?"

"Yeah."

I felt I had a fairly accurate mental representation of the inside of Justin's house now. He had previously been hiding in the den, which was directly beneath his bedroom. Adjacent to his bedroom was the master bedroom. I sensed the laundry room was located beneath that master bedroom—in the back corner of the first floor, most likely. Flanking one side of the den was the front foyer, which featured the front door with all the locks, and it seemed doubtful that Justin would have moved anywhere in that direction. An entrance into the laundry room henceforth had to be on the opposite side of the den somewhere.

All things considered, Justin was still in the wrong end of the house. The front door was in the foyer, while the garage door and rear sliding door were both in the living room at the other end of the house, all a long distance away. I gathered that the kitchen was a central area and a hub to many rooms. The kitchen very likely branched into the living room on the far side, the front foyer on the front side, and, ultimately, the laundry room on our side.

So it was the kitchen that stood between the majority of the escape routes. With two intruders to be wary of, it wasn't a safe place through which to travel. There were too many openings, doors, and corridors to be concerned with. The boy would need eyes on all sides of his head.

None of this mattered much anyway. The police were coming. Help was on the way. All we had to do was kneel on the football and run out the clock.

"Justin, I want you to stay where you are. You'll be safe in the dryer until the police arrive, okay?"

"Yeah," he mumbled in a low tone, which brought several thoughts to bear. I wondered how long he'd be able to endure such an uncomfortable enclosure. Before long, his neck would surely stiffen. And his cordless phone—how much longer would it last? Had the batteries been well charged? What would happen to him if his phone went dead?

Then another thought occurred to me.

"Justin? Justin, why did you move? What happened back there that made you decide to move to the laundry room?"

This suddenly seemed important. Given the circumstances, I saw little reason for a child to run the risks implied in changing hiding spots.

"I got scared they would find me back there," he said.

"But that man who was in the den left, didn't he? You said he went to the other side of the house."

"Yeah, but I started to hear things crashing upstairs, like the furniture and stuff. Upstairs in all the rooms."

"The other man in the upstairs, you mean? He was throwing furniture around?"

"Uh-huh," he replied. "And then the one down here started doing it too. I started to hear things crashing, like over near the living room where he went. Over there somewhere."

"So, while they were busy making all that noise, you chose that moment to change spots again," I realized aloud. I was recognizing the early tendrils of surprise creeping over me—surprise at the boy's courage and intelligence. I was about to commend him on this when suddenly the truth struck me.

"You mean you were worried they would come into the den and start tossing furniture around in there too. And maybe move the couch?"

"Uh-huh," he said. "They're looking for the safe."

I went stock-still in my swivel chair. A slow chill worked its way quietly through me. "Where is the safe, Justin?"

"I don't know. Mom wouldn't tell me."

"What's in it?"

"I don't know," he said. "She wouldn't tell me that either. All she told me is that we have a safe somewhere in the house."

How much more might the perps know? In addition to knowing of the engagement Justin's parents were attending, they had also known of a safe embedded in the house somewhere. And it was close to quarter of nine, I noticed. What dumb thief spends an hour burglarizing someone's home *unless he knows when the homeowners are coming back*?

A second, colder shiver rippled slowly up my spine, forcing me to lean back in my squeaky seat and reconsider things. There was much to reconsider.

"Can you still hear them, Justin? Moving the furniture?"

"Yeah. I think the guy down here is in Mom's good room."

"Don't worry about him, Justin. Stay where you are."

I doubted either of the intruders would feel compelled to look in the dryer. Anything was possible, though. If Justin were to accidentally bang his elbow or foot against the dryer wall, he could easily call attention to his whereabouts.

"The first man," I mentioned. "He's still upstairs, right?"

Justin paused. "Yeah, I think. Sounds like it."

"Any idea what room he might be in up there?"

"Uh-uh, over near the other side somewhere. Down by the study, maybe. I can hear his footsteps but not good."

"And the second man is still in the downstairs, you said?"

"Yeah."

There was little purpose behind these questions, I knew, other than me thinking out loud. Our best option—again— was to wait it out. Kneel on the ball. Wait for help to arrive.

But if those men are searching for a safe and don't find one, they may come to the laundry room. You know that, Leslie.

The perp would see the dryer. He'd see the door ajar and the narrow crescent of darkness revealed in that opening. He might not care. He might dismiss it and walk past. He probably wouldn't notice.

But he *would* arrive, providing the safe wasn't found. I couldn't discount the terrible danger, the opportunity for disaster. If either of the intruders chose to pass through the laundry room, Justin would be a precious arm's length from discovery.

I bit my lip, deciding that staying put was still our best option. It was surely safer than being behind the couch. One thing was sure: the intruder was smart enough to know that a safe wouldn't be hidden inside a dryer. He most definitely wouldn't think about opening the dryer door.

But what if he does, Leslie? What if the intruder wanders near and happens to see Justin peering out at him?

Stop it. You're being silly. The police are en route. We're minutes away from being out of this mess.

"Leslie?"

"Justin, you need to remain silent until the police get there. Are we clear on that?"

"Leslie, the lights just went out."

CHAPTER 8

MOST OF THE EVENTS that highlighted Richard's descent are nebulous to me now. Although I'm able to recall an accurate sequence of his downfalls, I can no longer depict exactly when those individual turnabouts took place with any degree of confidence. I am twenty-eight now. Four years have passed since his death, and even though I've done my best to try to cope with his loss, I've worked equally hard to put the entire mess behind me. I feel I've neared the point where the past no longer interferes with what's ahead, whatever that may be.

Somewhere along the line, Richard began using alcohol. It was near the time he was moved into finance, give or take several promotional rungs. In reflection, I don't believe the booze really worsened his disease. It merely accelerated the process. The problem was within Richard himself. Alcohol or none, he'd have hit bottom at one time or another. Though I failed to accept the predicament at the time, Richard was little more than a time bomb waiting to detonate. His drinking simply brought ground zero a little closer.

He established a small liquor cabinet for himself in his study, several feet from his desk. It was convenient, he said, because whenever he needed a drink, he could slide over to the bar on his wheel-mounted work chair and fix himself a number. That's what he began calling his drinks—numbers.

He'd throw a number together to relax; he'd have a couple of numbers and call it a night; one more number for good luck. I imagine he absorbed the lingo from some downtown bar, an assertion I'd have shamed myself for conceiving back then. But I'm a little older and a little wiser now, and I've come to realize that my failure to recognize the truth probably added as much fuel to the spreading fire as did his drunken ambition.

Which also leaves room for speculation concerning some of Richard's late arrivals from work. It's only logical to assume that he spent a lot of that "overtime" on a stool before a polished oak counter that I never knew about, downing some numbers with the guys. Shootin' the breeze.

Richard was learning the ropes of marriage and fatherhood from the score of omniscient patrons who took pride in the knowledge that they were tavern regulars. In truth, half of Richard's bar buddies probably weren't married, and the other half probably weren't fathers. And they most certainly didn't give a rat's ass about Richard himself or the crumbling life behind him or what he did with the bullshit advice they fed to him. All I know is that before long, my husband had a bar in his study and a sudden knowledge of how to mix drinks, and that he'd been one of the rare nondrinkers in college. But let's be honest. It's not the bar's fault or the daily clientele that infests it. Richard was the man who walked in there on his own two feet.

His use of the word *number* was likely a ploy to conceal what he was drinking. He never finished with a scotch and soda or a seven-and-seven or a dry martini. It was always a number. Perhaps it falsely boosted his ego, made him feel like one of the guys, one of the regulars. If so, I can only attribute this as another of Richard's failures. I'll never know how much time he blew off at that downtown oak counter, but I'm certain that he chose the wrong circle of friends in doing so. He looked up to the wrong people, struggled for inclusion in a group that only inserted more stones into the pool of concrete already swishing about in his head. Even today, I wonder how he fizzled off like he did, why he searched for acquaintances in a direction such as that one. He'd been one of the most self-reliant, self-confident, self-governing persons I had known back in school. Where things went wrong for him remains a mystery to me to this day.

Despite the addition of alcohol to his life, Richard never became a drunk, so far as I know. Perhaps things would have turned around for him if he had. Perhaps he'd have flirted with death with a soaring blood alcohol content one night and later undergone detox, forcing him to look himself in the mirror. Perhaps he'd have begun the AA program and turned his life around.

But those things never happened. Richard rarely drank to excess. He drank during the evenings, in his study, during long hours of paperwork. He drank slowly, to calm his nerves, to relax. Soon his numbers became his crutch for anxiety and tension, which simply shoved me farther away. And that was the problem, really. He came to me less and less for advice or company or solace. Instead, it was the glass by his blotter, with the elaborate stars and diamonds carved into the sides. He never quite became addicted to alcohol. He grew addicted to that glass, with what it did for him, with what it meant. The glass was like another woman to him, an adulterous intrusion that forged a space between us, one that grew wider with time. When the man I married needed comfort from the daily throes of the office, he chose his glass over his wife.

He'd come to bed later and later and would drop into sleep the moment his head hit the pillow. In the last six months of his life, I don't think we made love once.

*   *   *

On the day Patrick took his first step, Richard had an accident driving home from work. He dozed off on the interstate and drifted into the guardrail that separated the shoulder from a twenty-foot embankment. His Mercedes struck a post and caromed 180 degrees in a storm of sparks and crying metal. In midspin, a Volvo slammed into his rear just behind the back tire, which propelled the Mercedes the rest of the way through the one-eighty, and into the metal guardrail a second time.

Save for several bruises on his hands and arms and a mild laceration on the back of his neck from a shard of glass (the rear window had shattered), Richard was relatively unhurt. That little harm came to him is analogous, I think, to his not becoming an alcoholic. Just as booze could have handed him a ticket into detox and perhaps a recovery program, the accident could have landed him in a hospital bed.

And there he'd lay, my husband dressed in hospital whites instead of his three-piece suit. A fractured leg, internal bleeding, mild concussion, you name it. He'd be bedridden and immobile. There'd be no guarantees, of course, but one thing would be for certain: Richard would be forced to think. He would have more time on his hands than the previous two years put together and little choice but to use his brain for some introspection. Perhaps he'd try to sleep it off or watch some television … but the ulcer of free thought would come back to bite him. He'd stare out the window at the birds and trees and sky and would realize he'd forgotten what those things were, what they meant, and how they could be enjoyed. Eventually, he'd stumble upon the truth that he had done little thinking at all in the past years. He had simply *done*. And he'd discover that doing something for the sake of getting it done, without thought or enjoyment, was mindless, timeless, and unrewarding.

And he'd rediscover me. Me and Patrick. *Us.* He would refind us and remember that we were a family to which he had once belonged. One he had abandoned. This process would be painful, but it would be for the better.

But none of that ever happened with Richard. He didn't land in a hospital bed. He never faced himself in the mirror.

When I think back on it, I believe fate was taunting him, dangling a carrot in front of him, daring him to lunge. But Richard never lunged. Neither the alcohol nor the accident claimed him, and my husband never came to terms with himself.

What most infuriated me was his outright denial that anything was wrong. He came home that night with a tired, white pall on his face. He told me everything was fine. The accident was a minor setback, he admitted, but our insurance would cover the damages minus our deductible, and at least he'd come through unscathed. The truth is that he was hurt by being unscathed, as were Patrick and me.

"Rich, we need to talk," I told him that night during dinner.

"I told you, everything's been taken care of. The—"

"No, Richard. I mean us."

That silenced him for a moment. He stared at me across the table. "What's wrong? You think this isn't working anymore?" The irritation in his voice was palpable.

"Richard, you have to stop doing this."

"Doing what? Earning a living for us?"

"Is it worth it when you start falling asleep at the wheel?"

He threw a hard, granite look at me. He pointed and said, "Maybe *you* should mind your own business. *You*, who sits home all day while I bust my balls making—"

"Oh, Richard, that's bullshit, and you know it!" I cried, slamming my fist down on the table. "I have a child to take care of, so for God's sake, *stop acting like one!*"

That blew the fuse. Richard had been a clump of dynamite waiting to detonate. The accident had brought him precariously close but hadn't presented him a suitable target for venting his anger.

Without warning, he grabbed his plate of spaghetti and hurled it across the kitchen in a blind rage.

"You goddamn whore!" he screamed, jumping to his feet. "You fucking hightail bitch!" He grabbed his chair by the backrest and slammed it against the far wall. It made a tremendous *thwack!*—and something cracked in the works somewhere. I shrank back in my seat, horrified.

"I work my tired ass to the wall every fucking goddamn day, and what do you care? What do you do? You give me a fucking trip-ass attitude—like I'm not worth shit in a fucking baby's fuckridden Easter fucking bonnet! You fucking bitch!"

He leaned across the table, leering at me, firing his reckless exclamations at my face, spittle flying off his lips, landing on the food, the wood finish, on me, my shirt, my cheeks, like hot burning acid. The blood surged into his face, and he was suddenly as bright as a beet and darkening yet, turning purple.

"Bitch of a fucking whore is what you are, to say things like that!" Had I been closer, he may have grabbed me by the throat and begun choking me. Instead, he started grabbing anything he could lay his hands on, snatching them up and pitching them across the kitchen—into the walls, the cabinets, the microwave, the sink, the clock. He grabbed the condiments and threw them. The crystal salt and pepper shakers exploded against the window frame above the sink, sending a cloud of seasoning into the air and across the floor and counter. He found the bowl full of spaghetti and slammed it into the ceramic tile floor with disturbing force. The bowl shattered, and Ragu and linguine splashed wetly across the floor. He grabbed his placemat and threw that, grabbed the decorative flowers between us and threw those. The vase was Lenox. It bounced off the range and broke into thirty-three pieces when it hit the floor, scattering everywhere.

I watched with numb shock as my husband threw his tantrum, and his face grew darker, ready to blow up, and the drool dripped down his chin and neck, onto his shirt—already damp with the day's perspiration. He screamed and screamed with little Patrick, just under two years old, sitting beside me with two fingers in his mouth, eyes wide and confused. My husband grabbed the kitchen table, and Patrick started crying, really bawling. The wood table separated at the adjoining centerline with a pair of metallic clacks. My half collapsed, which sent my plate and glass of milk sliding to the floor. He yanked his half away and slammed it into the wall behind him, turned and kicked it, screaming and hollering, words I never understood, as loud as I'd ever heard him.

"I'm fucking sick of this! Do you hear me now? Now do you hear me? I am fucking fed up with this half-ass shit of yours!"

He kicked his half of the table again, again, again, until it cracked, splintered, and fell mercifully in half. He screamed once more at me, expelling another dollop of spittle onto the floor, then stormed out of the kitchen—food and broken glass strewn everywhere—up the stairs to his study where he no doubt poured himself a powerful number.

I sat in silence for a moment, hopelessly numb, Patrick crying beside me. Just numb. It was like I was nothing—just an amorphous, big black blob of nothing. I felt as though someone had reached inside me and turned me inside-out. Pins and needles were swarming through me.

Seconds later, my emotions surfaced. My eyes welled, and the tears burst forth with flood-like abandon. I remember dropping out of my chair because I no longer had the strength to hold myself in a sitting position. I crumpled onto the floor, in the spreading puddle of milk, and sobbed. I could hear Patrick crying above me, and for the one and only time in my life, I hadn't the strength to go to him. I lay in a weakly formed fetal position and cried until my eyes got sore. The puddle of milk expanded and rolled wetly beneath my cheek, and I didn't care. I hadn't the will to care.

When I found the strength to stand, I got Patrick and took him onto the back deck for a while. I rocked him until he fell asleep and then laid him down on the living room sofa. Then I returned to the kitchen.

I cleaned up the carnage in silence. Music from the kitchen radio would only mask the seriousness of the matter. I wept most of the way through and ruminated on how far below ground level my life had pin-wheeled. How much further could it go? The problem was nearly imponderable, and the dark future appeared to have no end, no solace in sight.

I was slow and weak. I felt gutted. It took me three hours to clean up the mess.

*   *   *

Three weeks later, a pair of Connecticut state troopers knocked on my door at one o'clock in the afternoon ... and I knew in my heart that Richard was dead. The day was hot and bright, and I opened the door for the troopers to walk through.

What unsettles me the most, I suppose, is the irony of the whole thing. Life is a crapshoot sometimes. Richard could have easily drunk himself into oblivion. He could have died at the wheel or from massive heart failure at the age of fifty.

But his death had little to do with his condition. He'd been out retrieving the mail, something he rarely did. Picture my husband, out in the dazzling sunlight in his thousand-dollar suit, granting himself a five-minute reprieve from the desk, the telephone, and the fountain pen. You'd think a higher power struck him down for breaking the pattern.

He'd been out at the mailbox when it happened. A delivery truck had swung wide making a turn, its rear wheels riding over the curb and onto the grass. To this day, it's a mystery to me how either the driver failed to notice my husband or my husband failed to get out of the way. It's one of those scenarios you run through your mind a thousand times, and it seems inconceivable with each run-through. But these things happen, I guess. Richard was clipped by one of the dual rear wheels and kind of sucked in. The driver never noticed and kept going. Richard's body was dragged five hundred yards along Industrial Avenue until a woman walking her poodle noticed the horrific sight coming toward her and motioned the driver to stop.

This may sound callous, but my many reflections on Richard's death conclude it to be a blessing in disguise. He may have died innocently, but his life was already spinning out of control. He was working ninety-some hours a week, drinking, not sleeping, not socializing, and eating himself away from the inside. His days on this earth were numbered. He'd have gotten shit drunk one afternoon and collided head-on with someone, killing others along with himself. Or he would have done himself in—I'm certain of that. One or two more years, and he'd have put a bullet through his skull, right in his own study, which would have sent me screaming for the sunset. And Patrick and I would have never received the insurance settlement that we did, which would have left us economically unstable.

I remember sitting in my living room that day, minutes after receiving the news. I wasn't heartbroken or dreadfully sad or really even shocked. Somehow, a part of me had been expecting it. Just not like this. More than anything, I was numbed by the implications: that my husband was gone; that Patrick and I were alone now; that Patrick would never know his father, however good or bad that was.

But the image that stuck most in my mind was that strip of Industrial Avenue, what it must have looked like, although I never did see it myself. It seemed impossible, even unworthy, that someone could die like that, much less my own husband. It seemed a paradox that all that blood could be trailed along the side of the road on a day bathed in glorious sunshine.

That was three days before Patrick's second birthday.

CHAPTER 9

"I HAVE TO MOVE." Justin's voice sounded cramped. "I'm moving now."

"What? Now? Why?"

Four to six minutes had passed since Justin had informed me of the lights having gone out in his house. I'd gone great lengths explaining to him that the power had not, in fact, been lost. Had this been the case, his phone would have shut off. A cordless phone did not behave like its noncordless predecessor. A cordless phone had a base unit that relied on electricity. Unplug the base—or cut off power to it—and you lost the signal existing between the base and the phone itself.

I'd taken the time to explain that one or both of the intruders had very likely heard approaching sirens. They'd quickly gone through the house flicking lights off, hoping to thwart suspicion. It was possible they were fleeing the house entirely. For all intents and purposes, our cat and mouse game was nearly over. One final kneel-down as the clock reached zero.

"Justin, wait … just a few more minutes is all—"

But already I could hear him moving, using his arms and legs to climb out of the dryer. "I can't stay here anymore. My neck hurts too much. It really hurts."

"Oh, Jesus. This is a bad idea. Justin, I wish you wouldn't do this. Can you even see where you're going?"

"I don't need to see."

"Oh God, Justin, please be careful. And keep your voice down."

"I will."

"Are you sure it's safe?" I asked. "Is one of those guys still downstairs?"

"In the den, I think," he whispered. I visualized him with that Cyclopean eye in my mind, saw his head cocked to one side in the darkness, listening intently for any sounds or footfalls emanating from his den.

And he was hearing something. I grew nervous by the mere fact that I couldn't hear it with him, that I was excluded. I suddenly feared that Justin's sense of caution had waned. An hour ago, he'd needed convincing to move at all. Now he was moving at will against my counsel. He was trading hiding spots with little or no fear, bouncing through the house as though a harmless game of tag was all this amounted to. I felt more helpless now than ever before.

"What's going on, kid?" I asked.

"Oh, Leslie, he just moved the couch," Justin whispered. A shiver shuddered my bones. "The one I was hiding behind bef—"

"Okay, that's enough," I told him forcefully. "Stop talking and go to tap, and move to wherever you planned on going."

The police had to be getting nearer. The sirens had to be spiraling closer. Any minute now, they'd be knocking the door down. So why weren't the perps leaving? Did they not know what was best for them? Did they honestly think that dousing the lights would inure them from discovery?

I recalled my mental image of Justin's house and remembered that the den was somehow linked to the laundry room. And that the laundry room was somehow connected to the kitchen. And the kitchen was the center point, from which one could travel to any door …

"Are you moving now, Justin?"

Tap-tap.

He's tiptoeing, is what he's doing. Walking slowly, softly.

"Just keep yourself quiet," I told him. "Are you going toward the kitchen?"

Tap-tap.

"Where are you? Are you there yet?"

Tap.

I figured there was a hallway of some sort, perhaps even a room, that adjoined the laundry chamber to the kitchen area. Maybe a simple corridor with a bathroom along the way.

Justin was traversing this passage right now. I employed my Cyclopean vision and saw him arriving at the junction to the kitchen. All was dark and motionless.

He was listening for movement: alien sounds in distant regions of the house; the guy upstairs; the guy in the den. I envisioned Justin standing gingerly, ears pricked to the height of alertness.

Come on, Justin, sit down already. That guy in the den scared me the most. He could react to any sound Justin made and run into the kitchen via the front foyer or come through the laundry room to grab the boy from behind.

"Are you in the kitchen yet?" He had to be. He *had* to be.

There came a lengthy pause that reeked of loud thought before he replied, tap-tap … and through an unspoken mental connection we now shared, I was suddenly seeing through his eyes, experiencing his darkened world for myself. I knew his mouth was open wide because mine was as well. I knew his heart was pounding because so was mine. Together we had arrived at a threshold.

The basement door. We were staring straight at it, the two of us. We couldn't see it in the darkness, but we both knew it was there. We both understood in a fundamental manner that it perhaps represented the best escape route out of this place.

But we first had to get there. And we had to do so without tripping over our own feet. *And don't forget about the island counter. A mad dash to the door won't cut it. We've got to work our way around the island counter in the dark and then feel our way to the door. And then, sweet Jesus, we have to get that door open. Turn the knob and pull it open ... and what kind of noise will that make? I'll bet the hinges squeal like rusty hell.*

How did I know Justin's kitchen had an island counter in it? Or that the basement door was closed? I don't know how I knew. Somehow, I just knew. The self-assurance of my thoughts neither alarmed nor surprised me.

"Is it the basement door, Justin? Is that what you're staring at?"

Tap-tap.

"The door is closed, though, isn't it?"

In a fierce whisper: "The lights are coming on again, Leslie."

What?

"Don't stand there, Justin. Get behind something. Go underneath something. *Hide.*"

"Where?"

"Anywhere. For God's sake, get out of sight."

He began moving—which way I don't know. I hoped he wasn't going backward, into the laundry room again. Was he advancing into the living room, perhaps? There were two known escape routes leading out of the living room. I considered coaching him in that direction, but before I could do so, I heard him huffing and panting, and I knew he was crawling into a new spot, the cordless phone tucked between his ear and shoulder.

"What's happening, Justin? Are you in a new hiding place now? Tap back to me if you are."

Moments later, tap-tap.

I hesitated, trying to devise a way of asking where he was with a yes or no question.

"Are you still in the kitchen?"

Tap-tap.

He hadn't crossed the room, then. He had not entered the living room.

"Are you out of sight?"

"I'm under the sink," he whispered. "In the cabinets by the floor."

"They can't see you, can they?"

"Uh-uh, the cabinet door is shut. It's really dark in here."

"Maybe you shouldn't speak," I told him. "They might hear."

"I don't think so. I can hear if somebody comes close. Leslie, I thought the police were coming. You said they were coming."

"I know, Justin, I know. And they *are* coming, I promise you. We may need to be a little more patient than we earlier thought. But that means you have to stay put. No more going out on your own. Is that understood?"

"Why did the lights come back on?" he asked.

"Justin, I don't ... I really don't know what's going on ..."

I was distracted by Sam Evans and Patty Lunesta. Both were gathered beneath the Fischer again. Both wore gravid faces. I heard bits and pieces of David Block's play-by-play voice, mingled with the voices of other volunteers, and moving chairs, and Justin talking to me in one ear. "Time out, Justin. Hold on a second." Block had just mentioned something about an accident. I had to assume it was the aforementioned collision on Route 7 to which he was referring—the one involving the Greyhound bus. But moments later I heard the words *Orchard Drive* issuing from the speakers, so this must be a new one.

Orchard Drive was a road I knew well. As a matter of fact, it wasn't far from the church. It was a treacherous stretch of County Road 519 that wound its way through the sloped, angled terrain of the Wortman's apple orchard. The road was characterized by tight, looping S-turns and low visibility. And because the road was elevated well above ground level, accidents and spinouts were common. It was not unheard of for a fast-moving car to fly off the road and come to rest, ensnared, in the upper limbs of an apple tree.

David Block had added Orchard Drive to his growing list of roads now closed for the night.

I had to get on Orchard Drive in order to get home. If it was closed …

I'd have to go another way, that's all. Certainly, there were ways around the orchard, but those routes were circuitous and time-consuming. Crestfallen, I began to think less of Justin and his parents and more about Patrick and Tammy and the steps I was going to have to take in order to get home that night.

You may not be getting home at all, Leslie. First things first. Take care of Justin. You can call Tammy later.

"You think your parents might be home soon, Justin?" I asked. "It's almost nine."

"Don't know. I told you, they didn't say."

"Do they usually get back late when they go out like this?"

"Sometimes."

"Sometimes what?" I asked. "What's that mean?"

"I don't know. Sometimes they get back real late. Like after I go to sleep in my bed."

"What time do you usually go to bed?"

"I don't know. Whenever I feel like it, I guess. Ten, mostly."

"Do you hear them usually, when they come in?" I remembered the spiral stairwell that linked his room to the den, which neighbored the front foyer.

"Yeah. Mostly. I'm mostly too scared to fall asleep until they come back."

"I can't believe they leave you home like this," I told him, no longer bothering to hide my displeasure. "I'm not surprised that you're scared at night, Justin. If I were a kid, twelve years old even, I'd be scared too."

Silence for a moment. I grew anxious at first but then forced myself to relax. The boy was simply thinking, that's all. And thinking loudly.

"Well, it's a good thing you know our number, huh, Justin?"

"Yeah," he replied in a far-off voice. I sensed he was devoting only a fraction of his attention to me, the rest to something beyond my knowing. Loud thought if I ever heard it.

"How often do you call us?" I asked. "I know you mentioned that you call in the afternoon most of the time, when I'm not here."

"Yeah, mostly. Not much to do around here. Except watch TV and stuff."

He'd dropped into that pensive mode again, as he'd done the two previous times I had addressed this subject. I was now certain that he was holding onto something, keeping his fists balled tightly around it. Over the phone, to a person he'd never met, I couldn't expect much. But kids are like that. Something bad happens, and they hold onto it, afraid to let it go, or perhaps believe it. They're at an age where good and bad means little because they've yet to be fully taught what is *good* and what is *bad*.

But one thing is unmistaken. They leave clues behind. I've seen this many times. They leave hints of an inner turmoil that oftentimes not even they comprehend. Though incapable of accurately articulating their distress, they almost always leave a scent trail behind them. It is the job of the parent or caregiver to pick up on the scent and follow it to its source.

I tried to visualize Justin's parents. I really couldn't see them as the type to pick up on their son's distress signals. This may have had something to do with the fact that they'd left him home alone after dark in a snowstorm.

Follow the scent, Leslie …

Most of our calls *were* the result of latchkey boredom. Most kids wanted someone friendly to talk to, someone to confide in. Justin was no different. But much of this work is intuitive. Sometimes it was best to listen to your gut.

Follow the trail …

"Are you sure there isn't something else you want to tell me, Justin?" I asked him. "Something at home? Or something at school that's bothering you? It could be one of your classes, or maybe a bully on your bus?" I was greeted with phone static. "I won't even talk if you don't want me to. You can tell me, and I won't say a word. Promise."

I was greeted with more silence, more loud thought.

Although I was doubting my chances of locating the source of Justin's discontent, I decided to take a small gamble by saying nothing. I greeted his silence with a silence of my own. I sat and waited. I would force him to issue the next word, whatever that might be.

There was a lot of static and a great many wheels turning in his head, but I held my ground. I drummed my fingers on the scarred desk surface. I glanced across at Mary, whom I'd nearly forgotten. I saw my own weariness mirrored in her complexion and wondered how many calls she'd fielded during the course of *this* call … and whether she had any inkling of how long this call had lasted. I was already over an hour, which was easily a personal record. The existing record for lengthiest call at our station was two hours and twenty minutes. The recipient of that dubious honor was a volunteer named Stacey Dour, an older woman who is no longer among our staff. It was dubious because no one had ever verified who exactly she'd been on the phone with for those two-plus hours. Back then, calls had not been recorded as they are today. There were several prevailing rumors pertaining to Stacey Dour's mystery caller the day she'd set her record for longest call. One theory maintained that she'd been on the phone with a ten-year-old boy whose older sister had been giving birth on the kitchen table. Another held that she'd actually been conversing with her divorce lawyer the entire time. A third rumor—

"I'm scared … I don't know. Just scared."

My reverie died in its tracks. "Scared of what, Justin? Scared of who?"

"Mrs. …" He paused to swallow a lump in his throat. "Mrs. F-Fallon."

"Who is Mrs. Fallon, Justin? Want to tell me about her?"

"My teacher," he said.

"You're scared of your teacher? Why?"

There came a long, anxious pause before he continued. "She's not … nice … to me anymore."

"Mrs. Fallon is mean to you, you're saying?"

"I'm scared of her."

"What does she do that you don't like?"

"I don't know. She doesn't like me."

"Why, Justin? Why doesn't she like you?"

"She told me to get out," he said.

"Get out of what?" I asked. "Out of her classroom?"

"She told me to shut up. She thinks I'm bad."

"Why does she think that, Justin? Tell me."

"But I didn't do anything. It wasn't my fault."

"What, Justin, *what?*"

He hesitated, perhaps to regather himself and his thoughts. Maybe to realign himself with the situation at hand. Maybe anything. It was the loudest thought I ever heard.

"We had half-days for a whole week," he said. "'Cause our parents had to talk to our teachers."

"Parent conference week," I said. "That was last fall, right?" Our afternoon staff had supposedly been busy that week.

"Yeah, I think. But my dad, he picked me up from school the one day and dropped me and Joey off at the playground."

"Okay."

He halted again, and I feared he'd reached a critical point … that he might abort his entire story right here.

"What about your dad?" I asked. "Did he stay at the playground with you?"

"Uh-uh. He went back. He went back."

"Back to the school?"

"Yeah."

"For the conference, right?"

"Yeah."

"What about your mom? Did she go to the conference too?"

"Uh-uh," he muttered. "She had to work a lot."

"Your mother was working?"

"Yeah."

"All right," I said. "So what happened? Something happened to you at the playground?"

"My dad said he would pick me and Joey up later, but Joey got hurt."

"Joey got hurt after your dad had already gone," I restated, to be sure.

"Yeah. We were on the big slide, going down it, and he got hurt."

"What happened to Joey?"

"He cut his leg sliding down one time. Something sticking out on the slide cut his leg open, and he was bleeding real bad and crying real loud."

"And you couldn't call your dad because he wasn't home," I said. "He was at the school."

"Some lady heard us and called a policeman."

"And the policeman came and got both of you?"

"Uh-huh. We had to go to the hospital so Joey could get stitches from the slide."

"Was Joey all right?"

"He was crying a lot 'cause he was really scared. His dad and mom came to the hospital to get us."

"Right," I said, trying to follow the story. "So, what happened next? Did you get home okay?"

"Yeah, 'cause Joey's mom and dad dropped me off."

"Oh, I see now. Now you were at home, but your father was still supposed to pick you up at the playground, right?"

"Yeah."

"So, what did you do? Did you try to call the school or tell Joey's parents?"

"I forgot until I got in my room."

"So, you didn't tell Joey's parents, then."

"Uh-uh. I got scared and tried to call the school 'cause I was afraid my dad would get real mad and punish me."

"And what happened when you called the school?" I asked.

I was greeted with silence, and I knew I was on the threshold.

Open your fist, Justin. It's all right …

"I h-had to go over to my mom and dad's room 'c-cause they have the cordless phone and a … phone book in there … to call … the school."

"It's okay, Justin, it's okay. I'm right here with you. I'm right here."

"The d-d-door was closed going in there, and I opened it … to go in … and … I saw …"

Oh my God, no … I covered my mouth, breathless.

"—my dad on the bed—"

—*Oh, Jesus*—

"—and he saw me—"

—*no, don't say this*—

"—and … and … sh-she was sitting there—"

—*no, no, no*—

"—with no … clothes, and … and sh-she turned around, and … it was Mrs. Fallon, and she yelled at me real loud to g-get out—"

The boy dissolved into tears, sobbing gently into the receiver. As far as I saw it, he had no more to say.

I was devoid of words. A numbing grayness had swelled within me, and I swayed from its drunken effect. I couldn't remember having felt this powerless since Richard had thrown his tantrum in the kitchen and I'd been unable to tend to Patrick's crying. How does one respond to something like this? How does one justify it, sum it up, cast it in a better light when there is nothing to justify, nothing to sum up, and no light to extenuate the ugliness of the wrongdoing? I couldn't even hug the child, which was what he needed at that moment more than anything. I could do nothing at all. It was just him and me and a phone line between us.

"I'm … sorry, Justin." It was weak and inadequate, but it was all I could muster. "I'm so, so sorry."

CHAPTER 10

NINE O'CLOCK STRAIGHT UP. The close-down process began around me. I caught a glimpse of Luetta Saxton, a gorgeous, dark-skinned woman, as she bundled herself beneath a thick overcoat, waved to several people, gave Sam Evans a hug, and trounced out the door into the outer reaches of the church basement. Mary was still handling a call across from me.

Justin wept for several minutes, and I stayed with him, consoling him as best I could. There was little I could do, and crying it out was probably the best remedy anyway. He at least knew that what he had seen was wrong and that it felt better to get it out.

Until now, he had told no one of his father's infidelity—not even his mother, whom he feared telling. And the stress he faced in school was obvious. I envisioned him sitting in his classroom with Mrs. Fallon glaring down at him, not to mention his father on the other side of the problem, at home. I couldn't imagine how the boy had coped up to this point. I was equally surprised he hadn't repressed the event and that he'd been capable of articulating it to me, a stranger.

"I'm so very glad that you told me, though," I said. "This is an awful thing you've seen, and it's important that you were able to tell someone."

"Uh-huh." He sounded ashamed for having witnessed such a thing.

But I could *feel* the cleansing he'd undergone, the removal of that tremendous weight from his chest.

It was imperative, of course, that Justin bring this matter to his mother, but I left that issue alone for now. To be perfectly honest, I wasn't sure that Justin's revelation of his father's afternoon fling would be conducive to Justin's physical and mental well-being. What if his mother refused to believe him? And his father later beat the tar out of him?

You need to let that go for now. There's only so much you can do, Leslie.

"Ow," the boy said suddenly.

"What? What was that for?"

He groaned. "Bumped my elbow in here."

"You all right?"

"Uh-huh."

"Be careful of the plumbing pipes under there. They're all metal."

"They're farther down, I think. By my feet. The sink is over my feet."

"Well, whatever, just be careful," I told him. "Don't bang against anything too loudly. You need to stay quiet."

"I know. They didn't hear me."

"What's happening over there anyway? Can you still hear those men?"

He paused. "Uh-huh. They're upstairs, I think."

"Upstairs? *Both* of them? Can you hear them?"

"I think," he whispered. "They're still moving things around."

I wondered what Justin's house was going to look like when those perps got finished with it.

And what a surprise the mister and missus are going to have when they walk in. Whenever the hell they get back, that is.

"This is up to you, Justin, but do you think you might want to try and get out of the house now? Through the basement?"

He chewed on that for a moment, which signified his unease.

"You don't have to if you don't want to."

"I don't know. I'm still afraid a little, about the basement."

"I know what you mean. There's probably no one else down there, but you're not sure."

"Uh-huh."

"Plus the fact that you feel okay where you are right now. Right?"

"Yeah, I guess."

"Up to you," I said. "If you feel safer sitting it out, that's fine with me. I'll sit it out with you."

I waited for him to say something in return, but he didn't. I figured he was pondering my idea. More loud thought.

"In fact," I told him, "if we're going to use this approach, we'd best go to tapping."

I waited for him to comply, but I was greeted with silence. I held onto the phone and listened, opened my mouth to speak but then shut it. I treaded water in the moment, hearing raspy static through the phone line and the thumping at the sides of my neck.

Something is happening ... something in his kitchen.

It was just like before, those other times when the boy had suddenly lapsed into silence. The ensuing quiet was no different here, and I intuitively knew to keep my mouth shut. Through a wavelength we now seemed to share, I perceived Justin crammed beneath the counter space, having tuned me out in order to tune in to an alien sound in the kitchen or somewhere else close by.

Maybe his parents are walking in, I wondered with thin hope, knowing this wasn't the case. Finally, I opened my mouth to ask in my softest voice—

I froze when I heard a noise through the receiver.

A faint sound was coming through ... barely audible ... barely perceptible. It was almost smooth—if, in fact, a sound can be described as such. Susurrant ...

What's going on? What is that noise? What is Justin doing?

I was frightened by not knowing, unable to plan a course of action. My pulse throbbed louder in my neck. I could feel my heartbeat jabbing the inside of my ribcage.

I was here in the church basement, yes ... but I forced myself out of these surroundings, squeezing everything into the phone world, into that claustrophobic counter space, and listening intently.

The sound paused, then resumed. And now I heard a low, rhythmic clicking embedded within the sound.

"Justin, are you okay? What's happening? What is that noise?"

Answer me, dammit. Answer me.

"Justin, please—"

"My elbow hit it again. It was my elbow."

"What, Justin, what? Tell me what you—"

But then the sound came again, low and clicking and rhythmic, and I suddenly recognized he was turning some sort of a dial ... and then there was a silence between us, and I think we both knew what he had found.

CHAPTER 11

HELPING LATCHKEY CHILDREN IS something I've wanted to do for years. Only now, with Richard four years dead and Patrick in first grade, am I able to volunteer some of my time. I'm back at my accounting firm working five hours a day while Patrick is in school. The firm is the only plausible reason for us having remained in Sheldon following Richard's death. They agreed to reopen their doors to me once Patrick started school, and during the hours I requested. Thus, I can be home during the afternoon when Patrick gets off the bus. I am able to put in three nights a week here, which is fantastic. Tammy Culberson babysits regularly, and things work out just fine.

My interest in helping latchkey kids was sparked when I was a teenager. It was my childhood friend Becky who sparked it. Becky was worse than latchkey. The more time I spent with her, the more I learned that she was flat-out neglected.

Becky occupied my house, I think, more frequently than her own. She once told me she enjoyed my place because good things happened there and people smiled. I never went to her house much but, based on her words, gradually garnered a feel for it. She had two older sisters who were incessant drug users and parents who, according to her, were constantly feuding. They divorced eight months following her accident.

Becky and I were friends, but she may have had the lowest self-esteem of anyone I'd ever met. She'd often mumble things instead of saying them outright and with any confidence. When asked to repeat something, she seldom would, more often than not discarding it. She was overly apologetic and devoid of ambition. I became slowly convinced that Becky didn't believe in herself and that it was her parents' fault.

My method of helping her was simply being with her and being her friend. I assured myself it was the best I could do at my age, owing to the fact that the real problem was in her home, not in her. I couldn't waltz into her house, wave a magic wand, and make things better.

Becky and I often sat on the bridge above the train tracks not far from where we lived … and that's where it happened, and that's how I came to regret my passive approach in helping her. Earlier tonight, I had told Justin that Becky's sandal had slipped off her foot one night when she and I had been sitting on the bridge. But that really wasn't the truth. It wasn't Becky's sandal that had slipped off her foot. It was Becky who had slipped off the bridge. Dusk was fast falling, and we were lifting ourselves up to stand—to stand, then turn around and grab hold of the iron girder and traverse the concrete ledge back to solid ground. And then return home.

But then disaster struck. We were halfway to our feet when suddenly Becky's hands slid out from underneath her. She kicked once and went feet first over the edge, screaming.

I have replayed that scene a thousand times over in my memory, as seen through my peripheral vision. Becky on my right: slipping, falling, screaming. Slipping, falling, screaming.

Slipping, falling …

She still screams today, seventeen years later. Like an instant replay camera, I can slow down the film in my memory and analyze each successive movement, from the second she lost her grip to the moment she disappeared over the edge. It took years for me to realize that Becky slid off that overhang herself. She *meant* for her hands to lose their purchase while we were standing up. She didn't accidentally lose her grip, but *forfeited* it. From the corner of my eye, I can still see Becky propping herself partway up and then letting herself fall. What scares me the most in hindsight is that we sat there talking the entire evening, and it was me doing most of the talking. I know now that Becky probably wasn't listening. As I prattled on about boys and music videos, my friend sat silently beside me, lost in her own head as she planned out her suicide.

I watched in horror as she plunged to the bottom, arms and legs wheeling, screaming. She landed between the rails with a smacking thud that echoed up and down the railway gorge. I heard bones breaking. In the silence thereafter, I became aware of myself sitting again, looking down, agape, as a ribbon of drool crept down my chin. Becky had landed at a severe angle, with her torso and upper body contorted upward, facing the sky. Her mangled legs were twisted to one side, away from her body. Her mouth and eyes were open. And for one dark and terrible moment in the descending gloom, we seemed to be staring at each other.

I remember climbing to my feet and scrambling lengthwise along the ledge without holding onto the girder. The steep embankments on both sides of the railroad gorge were festooned with brush and briar bushes, and suddenly I was battling my way through them, thrashing and clawing and kicking and waving. When I emerged onto the tracks moments later, my skin had been laced open in multiple places on my legs, arms, hands, face, head, and neck. The scratches hadn't yet begun to sting. I approached Becky's disfigured body and felt my gorge rise in my throat. Both of her legs were broken. I could see one of the fractures in her left thigh, where the stump of her broken femur was making a grotesque bulge in the skin. One of her arms lay across the rocks in an impossibly crooked position, her forearm bent the wrong way from the elbow. The fingertips of that hand were jittering with some sort of postmortem reflex. Blood was running from her nose and mouth, forming crimson rivulets that trickled down her cheeks and past her neck. Another pool of blood was spreading around the rocks beneath her head, and although that side of her skull was against the ground, it was dreadfully apparent that it had cracked open.

I stood over her, webbed in a medley of shock, disbelief, and horror. I remember thinking, *This is my friend. She's right here on the tracks at my feet, and she's dead, and I saw it happen, I saw her fall, I saw the whole thing—*

That's when I heard the wheezing sound. All thought processes halted inside me. I stood frozen above her, listening. Right away, I knew what I didn't want that sound to be ... and I knew that that was exactly what the sound was. I knelt down, my pulse a drumbeat in my neck as blood from the countless scratch marks began streaming down my legs ... and I saw that Becky was *breathing*. Thin, raspy breaths were escaping her just-parted lips, and her chest was barely moving up and down. She seemed not to acknowledge my presence. She stared past me into the deepening sky with an animal fear in her eyes.

This girl is alive, I remember thinking. *After all that, she's still alive. Not by much and maybe not for long ... but God and Jesus, she's breathing.* That scared me the most because I suddenly had to act, and act fast. I had to do something, anything, because every passing second was now a grain of sand sliding through the hourglass.

The next moment I was charging through the prickers again, only going uphill this time, oblivious to the thorns slashing at my face and neck and knees and wrists. And suddenly I was in the middle of the interstate. Not on the shoulder, mind you—in the *middle.* I was jumping up and down and waving my bloody arms like a crazy person, inciting a bedlam of car horns, screeching tires, and irate faces. Several drivers never stopped but maneuvered past me instead, shouting and showing me their middle fingers. It was a woman in a pink maternity dress who got out of her Volkswagen first and peered over the chipped concrete railing as per my pointing and panicked babbling. A slew of vehicles amassed behind her, and soon the interstate was clogged all three lanes across, people screaming out their windows and blaring their horns. A burly, beard-ridden truck driver clambered up to the scene next to me and the woman in the maternity dress, his face sweaty and grimy. He bent over the railing next to us, and two toneless words escaped his lips: "Holy shit." And then he was gone, swashbuckling back to his truck, where I knew he had a radio. I heard sirens minutes later, zeroing in from all points of the earth.

It's amazing how quickly a crowd will gather around another's misfortune. Before I knew it, ten, twenty, then thirty-some onlookers were clustered atop the concrete bridge, peering over the edge in fascinated horror. The interstate was chaotic, with cars everywhere and people yelling and pointing. Strobes and flashing lights appeared from all directions. Emergency vehicles were forced to access the scene from the other side of the highway because of the tremendous jam. Soon they were crossing the median in waves. It was nearly dark by that time, but the night was turned red.

All was a blur for me from that point on. The shock really set in, and the maelstrom of stimuli around me began to numb my senses. For this I am grateful.

Becky was medivacked to Fairview Memorial Hospital, and I was escorted to police headquarters for extensive questioning. Based on my description of Becky's fall and from many answers I provided to countless questions that essentially asked the same thing in different ways, it was concluded that Becky's fall was a tragic accident. Only years later, having reseen the event time and again have I arrived at what I'm sure is the truth.

Is there an opposite of a "miracle"? Does such a word exist in our terminology, much less the spectrum of our understanding? We often define a miracle as an event of extraordinarily low possibility that is *good*, so very good—perhaps even God sent. It is the *goodness* of the happening that makes a miracle what it is.

But how about this identical scenario with horribly bad consequences? We can't call it a tragedy, really, because tragedies happen every day, all over the world. We see them on the news and read them in the paper. Some say there is a miracle to offset every tragedy in the world, but I'm a disbeliever of this sentiment for reasons that I won't divulge here.

Whatever the case, Becky's "accident" was the stark opposite of a miracle *because she survived.* Her survival may have been a medical and bodily miracle. But surviving never meant much to Becky, before *or* after the accident. All it meant, when you got down to it, was that she breathed, ate, and slept. Becky had tried to end her life that night on the concrete bridge, and she failed. It was extraordinary that she failed given a fall like that, and anything but a miracle.

Becky broke her one arm that I described and both of her legs—one of the legs in two places. It was her legs that partially broke her fall, which somehow prevented her spine from snapping and most probably killing her.

The skull breakage I thought I had seen was, indeed, just that. She cracked her skull along her left temple, just above the ear, which resulted in a rare and complicated head wound. The fracture severed her middle cerebral artery, which led to an epidural hemorrhage. The hemorrhage, little different than a tumor, exerted damaging pressure to the left side of her brain. The hemorrhage was repaired surgically, but Becky was left with a permanent hemiplegia: she was paralyzed on the right side of her body. Because the nerves in the brain cross over via the corpus callosum, the left side of the brain essentially controls the right side of the body and vice versa.

From Fairview Memorial, Becky was admitted to the Goldrise Clinic, a facility for the mentally and bodily impaired, forty miles from her home. The clinic was state funded despite its fancy title. There Becky remained for the rest of her life.

Her parents divorced eight months following her fall, and her family just seemed to blow away like leaves on a street corner. Her mother and one of her sisters—one who did, in fact, eventually seek recovery from addiction—went to see her occasionally, but their visits, to the best of my knowledge, tapered off to almost none once two years had passed. Becky's only real supporter was a great uncle who went to see her every month or so, a man I never met. Three or four years after the fall, however, this lone, caring relative died in his sleep one night, and then she had no one.

I visited her several times, three or four occasions perhaps, but eventually I stopped going as well. Becky degenerated through her five- to six-year stint at Goldrise. I tried my best to smile and, in turn, elicit one from her, to let her know I was still her friend. But it never worked. Becky couldn't smile back. The right side of her face was useless, and that side of her mouth seemed to sag. Beads of saliva were constantly dribbling off the paralyzed corner of her lips, and she used an old rag that she held to wipe her face every so often with her good arm. The optic muscles of her right eye had been impaired as well. When she looked at you, or anywhere else in her white clinic room, only her left eye moved, and *that* was borderline frightening. I was chilled, watching her good eye rotate robotically in her socket while the other, dilated and useless, stared straight ahead and down. This resulted in massive sight problems for Becky because now she was looking in two separate directions nearly at all times.

Becky's bad arm and leg were also withered. Her forearm, in fact, eventually crinkled up to a thirty- or forty-degree angle to her upper arm. One of the aides told me this was a flexion contracture. Paralyzed and useless, the muscles had retracted and pulled the forearm with it. I later learned that other private clinics with more resources kept the limb stretched to prevent the contracture. But Goldrise was a state job, where fewer nurses, of quantity and quality, were available. In such an institution, Becky was a lost cause.

Sitting there and trying to talk to her and trying to smile was a lie. All a lie, because it was an abhorrent experience. I cried my eyes out the first time I went to see her, ran into the ladies' room and sobbed. Seeing one of your friends bedridden like that, in such a miserable condition, will crack any living soul in the world. We'd been sitting on the bridge several months before ... and now *this*. It hits you hard, really goddamned hard, and then burns in you for a long time.

Becky could hardly speak. The right side of her mouth was useless, and everything she said was slurred and pathetic. The first time I visited her, she pronounced my name *Lethy*. There were bits and pieces of herself she never remembered. And for some reason, not once did I bring up the accident, which I knew was a suicide attempt. I always meant to ask what her intentions had been, but I never did. For some dark and painful reason that I can't explain and that I'll never understand within myself, I never did ask her.

After those three of four trips to the clinic spread over several years, I stopped going completely, and of this I am ashamed the most. It was a catch-twenty-two situation if I ever knew one. I felt indebted to her, the fact that I was her friend and that I'd been with her the night of the fall. But going to see Becky was a *horror*. It has taken me years to admit that. Going to see her stirred inside me every depressing and miserable emotion I have ever known—more so than Richard's death years later, even—and left me scarred and anguished for weeks to follow. Becky Finstead, once my friend, was now lost and pathetic and useless. Going to see her didn't help me or her. It was best to let her go, and that's precisely the worst of it. I've accepted that today but never forgiven myself for it.

Becky died in the Goldrise Clinic sixty-four months following her admission. I received word through the clinic itself and was inwardly relieved. It was best for Becky, better than her living hell, her suspended nothingness. She developed a cold that moved to her chest and grew to pneumonia. In her weakened state, she was unable to cough up her secretions, which dripped down and flooded her lungs. She essentially drowned in her own fluids, but her death was mercifully painless. She slipped into a coma and died quietly.

I was one of nine people at her funeral. My parents were two of them, as was Becky's mother and one of her sisters—the one who had sought rehab, I think. I never got it up to ask where the father or other sister was or what had happened to them.

The funeral was quick, and no one in the world heard a word about it. It was a gorgeous, sunlit morning. I didn't cry, not a tear, for there was little for me to be sad about.

I didn't hear what the tired, disheveled priest said as he read tonelessly from a tattered Bible and went through the funeral motions. I was a teenager, sixteen or seventeen, and

I eyed the small gathering and looked long and hard at the casket that contained Becky's body, suspended above her grave by a network of poles and straps. I remembered our nights on the bridge and other times and felt that old regret creeping back again. I remembered my passive approach to Becky's neglected life before the fall, my halfhearted commitment to help. I remembered thinking that there'd been little more I could do, and I felt sure of this knowledge all over again, six or seven years later. But I watched her casket and thought long and hard and deeply … and then stared into the sun for a while and wondered if I could have done something more. It's these types of things that take the many ropes of life and tie them into vicious knots. You can spend years trying to unravel them.

I believe my life turned during her funeral in a way I wouldn't realize until years later. I gazed into the sun that bright and beautiful morning and allowed much of my nagging regret to slip away. I left it behind, there on the funeral grounds at the foot of Becky's grave. *I'm sorry, baby. I'm sorry I couldn't save you. I won't let it happen again, baby doll. That's a promise.* I'd been just a kid when Becky had plunged, ultimately, to her death in the railroad gorge by our house. Given my age and inexperience at the time, I was unequipped to help anyone.

But things are different now. I'm twenty-eight years old, and now I can.

CHAPTER 12

"JUSTIN, YOU HAVE TO get out of there." My voice was taut.

"I'm scared, Leslie."

"I know you're scared, Justin. I'm scared too, but you can't stay there any longer. It's too dangerous."

"What if they find me?" His voice was tremulous.

"They won't find you, believe me. Not if they're upstairs. They'll never—"

"They might hear me, though. Opening the basement door to go down. It'll be too loud."

"Justin, we don't have a choice. You can't stay under the kitchen cabinet for another minute." I paused and then added, "You can make it. I know you can. The basement door is ten feet away."

"But, Leslie, the police, you said to wait for—"

"The police aren't coming, Justin. Do you understand? *No one is coming to help you.* If we're going to get out of this, we're going to have to do it on our own."

I remembered the jewelry box beneath the bed in the master bedroom. Justin and I, in a way, had come full circle, having returned to the predicament from which we'd started. Only this was different, and it was a whole lot worse. I thought, *That jewelry box meant little if you think about it. The intruders would have looked under the bed anyhow because they're tearing the goddamn house apart. That bed is probably upside down as we speak, with furniture strewn everywhere. Justin would have been discovered long ago, maybe even killed ...*

It was the safe those men were searching for. They were tossing chairs and sofas in all directions and ripping pictures off the walls. They were hunting for the safe and whatever valuable contents it enclosed ... and here it was, embedded into the back wall of the cabinet underneath the kitchen sink. Staying here any longer would be like hiding inside the treasure chest.

It was absurd, really—Justin's string of hideouts and the secrets they harbored. Each hiding spot had seemed to elicit a surprise from our collective thought, things we had refused to completely understand or accept in human terms. *Your own house can be like your own conscience,* I thought matter-of-factly. *You never learn what lurks in the corners until you squeeze into them for a close inspection.*

"Ten feet, Justin. All you have to do is go around that center counter, open the basement door, and go down the stairs."

"But they'll hear me opening the door—"

"No, they won't," I insisted, growing impatient. "They're upstairs moving things. They can't hear that far. Justin, you *have* to move. We have no idea when your parents are coming back, and those guys might keep looking until they *do* find the safe. Do you understand me?"

There was silence at his end as he channeled everything through his fevered brain—all I'd said, what was at stake, what lay ahead.

"Do you? It's important that you agree with me, Justin; believe me. I hate to make you do something you're afraid to do, you know that, but this is absolutely necessary."

He asked, "But what am I gonna do? I don't have shoes or socks on."

And I'm not gonna be able to get home tonight, I thought brutally, *so why don't you just quit your whining? Do you want to live to see tomorrow, or don't you? Because that's what this comes to.*

I bit my lip. "You're going to have to do the best you can, Justin. That's all I can say for now, and I don't think we have time to say much more. The snow will hurt your feet like you've never known, so you'll have to run as fast as you can to the nearest house. Can you do that?"

"But they weren't home, I told—"

"But that was over an hour ago," I pressed. "They're probably back by now. If not, break a window and get in, or run to the next nearest one. It doesn't matter *where* you go, Justin, as much as it does that you get out of *your* house. Does this make sense to you?"

"I think so," he said in a shaky voice. "I'm really scared."

"I know, Justin, but things will be fine. Trust me. Just stay quiet like you have all along tonight. You've been great up to this point."

"Should I go now?"

"Yes," I replied smoothly, softly. "Open the cabinet door, take a moment to listen to be sure the downstairs is clear, then step out softly. *Don't make a sound.*" I hesitated while those last words sank in. "Are you ready for this?"

"I think, I guess."

"Good. Remember, I'm right here next to you. We're in this together, right?"

"Uh-huh."

"Okay," I told him. "Go."

There was silence followed by an audible squeak as the cabinet door swung open. I recognized that inherent cabinet-door squeak right away. My Cyclopean eye assumed command, and Justin's kitchen seemed to unfold before me like a movie screen. At first there was a terrible, pulsing moment of revelation: the door swinging open, wider and wider ... and the child inside me was sure that a pair of filth-encrusted boots would be standing there blocking my way out, a towering hulk of a man looking down with a hard, unforgiving grin, as if he'd heard our conversation all along. The fear of this irrational premonition was quickly mitigated by an empty space of kitchen floor. No boots, no man glaring down. And a stealth silence coupled with the empty kitchen, queerly similar to a quiet before a storm. My Cyclopean eye saw through Justin's, and for one tense moment, we were sitting there as one, peering out from our sanction, listening alertly as we calculated the accessibility of the close but distant basement door.

"Everything all right?" I whispered. "They still upstairs?"

"Yeah," he whispered back, and that was all I needed. That singular word branched into a handful of perceptions for me. I imagined the thumping sounds of objects being moved on the floor above me, mingled with men's voices.

We're making this ten times harder than it is, I knew. *This should be easy. That door is right there, ten paces away ...*

"Okay, Justin. Step out now and quietly close the cabinet door behind you. Then tiptoe around the counter to the basement door. This should be easy. We're nearly free now."

I couldn't hear the cabinet door being shut, which was good, but I did see it. And I saw Justin glancing quickly over his shoulder. He looked one way, then the other, then back again.

It's okay, kid. You can make it, I know you can ...

And now he was creeping around the counter, that island in the kitchen. I saw him doing it, *felt* it. I perceived the cordless phone clutched in one hand against his ear, his free hand sliding across the smooth counter surface, as though to steady him or guide him, around, around ...

Almost there, Justin. Almost there ...

And now, around the corner with the closed basement door straight ahead, looming, *waiting* to be opened, and a new world waiting to be found. I sensed him pausing, one last apprehensive glance at the three entrances into the kitchen to ensure he wasn't being observed. A moment of trepidation and then the act, the act itself. In a way I'll never be able to explain, I knew exactly when the boy made that last make-or-break motion toward the door, and I don't think he took his eyes off it for a second. The rest of the kitchen—the entire house, for that matter—was pushed out of his mind, making that standing wooden door the sole object rendered in complete clarity.

He's there, I thought, and moments later I heard the knob turn. *Now he's turning the knob … and now he's opening the door … he's opening it … he's … yes, and now it's open, the door is open, and he's going down.*

"How we doing, Justin? Okay?"

"Yeah," he said in a half-panicked voice that revealed his heavy breathing. I heard his feet as he marched quickly down the steps, away from the kitchen, from the house, the lion's den.

And he left the basement door open above him, I knew suddenly, but I never bothered to mention it. Nothing, nothing, nothing in the world would have convinced him to go back up and pull it shut. True, the intruders might notice the open door and realize someone had escaped the house during their raping of it, but Justin would be long gone by then.

I was seized by the sudden impression of having been trapped in a dark tunnel all this time. Now, with the light at the end of the tunnel shining blessedly ahead, all our fear, worry, and caution were being suppressed by an overwhelming need to get out. My heartbeat accelerated with Justin's mounting fervor, which massed higher and higher with every step toward safety.

I no longer heard the soft thumping of stairs underfoot, so I gathered he was standing on the concrete floor of his basement. Standing there in his bare feet and …

"Justin? Justin, where are you? What's happening?"

I heard the sound of moving air. Justin's voice was raspy when he said, "They came in through the doors, the way I thought."

It took me a moment to realize what he was talking about: the Bilco doors were open. The intruders had left them open upon entering the house, and now Justin was staring at them. He was staring, too, at the pile of snow that had drifted on the basement floor and on each of the wood risers leading up, up, and out, where the doors yawned open to the night. The moving air that I heard was the wind of the snowstorm billowing in through the gaping escape hole.

Justin was standing locked in place, staring at his first visual evidence that his home had been entered.

"Justin, what are you waiting for?"

"It's cold," he said. I pictured him standing there in his bare feet, shivering.

"I know, but you've got to get out. Go to the nearest house and get in. I don't care if you have to use a rock to break a window."

"Yeah," he uttered in that shaky voice. In those final moments, I envisioned him peering up the stairs into his kitchen, then back to the open storm doors with the snow blowing in … then back to his kitchen. And now back to the storm doors.

"Run, Justin," I told him. "Run! *Now!*"

He did, leaving the kitchen and the basement, the perps, and all his clever hiding spots behind. I heard him moan and knew his first bare foot had touched the snow on the floor of his basement. The wind grew exponentially through the receiver. Moments later, it *howled.*

He's outside now; he's made it that far. He's climbed the stairs, and he's in his backyard.

"Don't waste a second, Justin!" I yelled, screaming to be heard. "Run fast! Go!"

The wind had to be powerful out there because it was shrieking through the phone line, making a high-pitched *sheee!*

"I am!" he answered, but I could barely hear him. His voice was a whisper over the storm's wrath. I winced as I imagined him, young, defenseless, and barefoot, holding a cordless phone as he trudged and stumbled through a Connecticut blizzard. I sensed, through the receiver, the icy chill against my cheeks. I felt the millions of bitter snowflakes stinging my eyes and face as the wind surged past me, so cold and numbing.

That incredible roar of rushing air continued, but as Justin moved farther from his house, away from the main phone housing, our reception deteriorated. Serpents of static began to leap and bound over the shriek of wind. Soon, I'd lose him completely.

My God, he'll be on his own out there.

"Justin!" I screamed. "Can you hear me?" Because my world was funneled into the raging phonescape, I hardly noticed Mary and the others staring wide-eyed at me here in the control room. "Justin, I'm losing you!"

Static hissed. His voice came through in disjointed slivers. "... can't h ... Leslie ... so cold ... I ..." More static. A gust of wind howled and drowned him out completely.

Oh God, you're losing him. He's moving out of range.

I suddenly felt helpless. If I couldn't hear him, it was a sure bet he couldn't hear me either. He was alone out there, somewhere in the state. If we got disconnected ...

The connection was weakening.

"Justin, where are you? Can you hear me?" I had the phone pressed against my face. I was hollering into it.

Static and wind, static and wind. A boy's voice, small and distant, sounding tens of thousands of miles away: "… ough fence t … yard … st there … eezing, Lesl … can't … l my feet …"

He's moving into his neighbor's yard, and he can't feel his feet. That's what he's trying to say.

"Keep going and don't stop!" I yelled slowly, trying desperately to be heard. "Go right up to the door!"

"… am … oor … should I just … in?"

"Don't even knock if it's open! Just get out of the cold! Do you hear me?"

Static lurched, and for a moment, I thought I'd lost him for good. The static was far greater than the howl of the wind now—louder, more frequent, longer. It hissed, crackled, spat. I heard fragments of Justin's voice slipping through but nothing more.

"… ere now … ta … le … ft … eet … sh … ome …"

I felt helplessness creeping over me like cold tentacles. I shuddered, shivered, bit down.

He's alone now, and he knows it. He's out there by himself, freezing to death, and he doesn't know what to do because he can't hear me. What can I do now? What can I do?

I flailed for reason, for an idea, for hope, for anything. My mouth hung open, waiting for something celestial to slide out … but what good would it be if he couldn't hear it?

He was talking a lot now—chips of his voice were slipping continuously through the static.

Think, Leslie, dammit, think. I know you can't hear, but just try.

I bit down hard, clenching the top of my scalp with my free palm, my brain in overdrive. They say the human brain is capable of climbing that one extra gear when dire necessity comes calling, and this was one of those moments. Everything was churning up there, working furiously, the wheels spinning and grinding, my pulse galloping, sweat streaming down my temples.

"… ome … do … o … ld … Les …"

He's talking a lot, which must mean he's there. He's on the doorstep, but he can't get in. That has to be it. He's there, and he's freezing …

"… obody … me … re … co … nd … ocked …"

That was it. My perceptions locked onto those initial sounds: … obody … me …

Nobody's home is what he's trying to say. He's trying to get through to you to ask what to do next.

A devil of wind roared him out. Static dragons sizzled.

I focused my efforts, squeezing everything I had into those dear, precious moments.

"Justin, can you hear me?"

"… do … ere … m free … ng …"

"Justin, get into the house any way you can! Get into the house! Break a window if it's locked up, just—"

I was interrupted by a clanging noise that came through the receiver, more prominent than his voice or the wind but garbled by static. I held my mouth open to finish my statement but placed my words on hold, trying to process the new noise. It was a repeating sound. Pounding, clanging …

He's banging on something. He's trying to break in.

The clanging was still there, loud and static-riddled, and I knew what it was, dammit, but couldn't bring it into conscious thought.

"Justin, what is—"

A pause, and then the sound resumed. He had noticeably stopped speaking, as if having realized that our connection was lost.

"Justin, what are you doing—"

The sound continued, again, again, again, and suddenly that huge lightbulb lit up in my head, and a million watts of insight flooded my vision.

He's pounding on the door. The door is locked, and he's knocking on it so hard it sounds like he's trying to knock it down. He's out there freezing, trying to get in, trying—

"Break a window, Justin! Break a win—"

My Cyclopean vision flashed bright and powerful all of a sudden, and I saw him standing barefoot in front of the locked door, and the vision was so crystal clear—

(*the human brain is capable of climbing that one extra gear...*)

—that I suddenly saw his hand fisted around one of those heavy, metallic door-knockers mounted to the heavy oak, and *that's* why the banging was so loud. So loud and heavy and clanging-like.

That one extra gear when necessity comes calling ...

His fist was clenched around it, snow swirling everywhere ... and suddenly, with an unthinkable power all its own, my Cyclopean eye flashed again, brilliantly, blindingly, and this time I saw too much. I saw a Bilco door, yes, a Bilco door, and a fence because he'd mentioned a fence, and I saw Justin standing on the front porch. Knocking, pounding, *pounding ...*

"Justin! Can you hear me? For God's sake, can you hear me?"

"... es ... dy hom ... er ... Les—"

Knock! Knock! Knock!

My heart was jackhammering, *thundering ...*

"Justin, what are you holding?"

"... an't ... in the ... se ..."

Knock! Knock! Knock!

"What do you have in your hand, Justin? *Answer me!*"

Knock! Knock! Knock!

"Is it a lion's head, Justin? Tell me! Are you knocking with a heavy lion's head?" My voice was strained to the max, and I felt every cord bulging from my neck.

Everyone was staring at me, gaping.

Knock! Knock! Knock!

"Goddammit, what is that? Are you holding a lion's head, Justin? *For God's sake, answer me!*"

My Cyclopean eye flashed again, and the picture was all too clear this time. A Bilco door, the fence, the yard …

A static demon screeched its hellish squalor but not enough to disguise Justin's disjointed reply.

"… *ess* …"

"*Oh my God, Patrick!*" I screamed at the top of my lungs, lunging to my feet and slamming the phone down. "*Oh my God! Oh my God!*"

"What's wrong?" someone was asking. People were staring at me, everyone, all of them.

I shot out of my swivel seat, slid it away from me, and pushed Mary out of my way, dashing for the coat rack in the corner by Mr. Coffeemaker.

"Leslie, Leslie, what is it?" All of them, asking at once.

"*Oh my God, Patrick! They got in my house! They got in my fucking house! Get out of my way! Everybody, out of my way!*"

I remember people yelling at me, remember seeing their concerned faces, and then I had my coat in my hands, I was throwing it on and digging for the keys in the pockets, searching desperately—

Then Sam Evans grabbed me by the shoulders and slammed me against the doorframe, his eyes beaming with a medley of anger, fear, and concern.

The wind was knocked out of me. I stared at Sam and tried to break loose.

"What are you doing? No, I have to go, Sam, I have to get to Patrick! I have—"

"You can't—"

"Let me go!" I yelled, thrashing, trying to break loose. "They broke into my house, dammit! They broke in, and no one answered the phone! They—"

"—out of here, Leslie—"

"—got Patrick, I have to—"

He squeezed his fingers into my shoulders, pulled me toward him, and slammed me into the frame again, harder this time.

The wind was again knocked out of me, and I saw stars now. My vision blurred, and I became dizzy. Through the haze and dizziness, I heard Sam's voice, soft and commanding. The wooziness cleared moments later, and I relaxed in his grip, staring at him and breathing hard.

"You can't go out there, Leslie. Can't you see we're all still here?"

I looked around fearfully and saw everyone looking at me. Luetta Saxton was there, a cup of steaming decaf in one hand, her eyes brimming. Her coat was off, and I suddenly knew why, but Sam completed the thought.

"It's a blizzard out there, Leslie. We're stuck here. We're snowed in for the night."

I panted helplessly in his grasp. "Oh my Go—oh my God, no."

I stood there for an awful, pressing moment, then tore free of his grip and ran back toward my desk. People parted to make way for me as I ran, their eyes wide and confused.

I got halfway there when the world seemed to land on my shoulders.

You hung up the phone, Leslie. Justin is gone. You broke the connection.

I stopped dead in my tracks and almost fainted. I stood there staring at my green phone, swaying one way, then the other. Dizziness reclaimed me.

You hung up. The connection is gone. You'll never get it back now.

I stood there for the longest moment of my life, and the room was dreadfully silent.

Oh my God. Oh my good Lord Jesus God.

CHAPTER 13

I COLLAPSED IN MY seat, panting and sweating, hands clasped around my head. I stared at the phone on my desk. The rest of the world seemed to have blurred out around it.

Think, Leslie. Think.

I felt panic chewing on me, threatening to eat me alive. I sensed I was teetering on the threshold, so perilously near to tipping. I was all nerves, blood racing, heart thumping, pulse beating. Falling over the threshold meant relinquishing all capability of rationale and action.

And *that* could not happen. Not now, here.

Patrick's life was in jeopardy.

You have to think. Keep your head in it.

I heard voices all around me, muffled and distant, strangely incoherent. It was just me, trapped in my own game. I snatched up the phone and punched in Justin's number. I got a busy signal. Justin's phone was essentially off the hook now. He wasn't aware the connection had been lost.

"Leslie, please tell us ..." Mary began.

"Mary, I don't have time," I blurted, slamming the phone down, my voice shaky. I refused to look up. "All of you, there's no time. There's a man in my house—or there *was* a man in my house—and Patrick is in danger."

Try calling home, Leslie.

I snatched up the receiver anew. My fingers quivered violently as I punched in my home number.

Relax, girl, relax. One button at a time now …

The line began to ring in my house, and a thousand thoughts roller-coasted through my head, mumble-jumbled like a tangle of spitting live wires. It rang twice, thrice, four times.

"Come on, Tammy, answer the damn phone. Answer it."

It rang a fifth time, a sixth.

Again, again.

No one's answering. This is my house. My son and the babysitter are there—supposed to be there—but no one is answering.

It rang a ninth time, a tenth …

"Were you on the phone with that one boy all that time?" one of the ladies asked, and I nodded nervously. Her eyes were deep with wonder.

"Keep all the lines open," I announced loudly. "Don't turn the recordings on. Justin might try and call back."

The line rang again, and again. My anguish climbed a notch with every ring.

"Mary," I said, still holding the phone to my ear, "get the state police on your line. Call the Sheldon barracks directly, don't dial 911. Tell them my house has been broken into. It's 19 Westfall Boulevard, second to last house on the left. Tell them my son and babysitter are inside. Then tell them where we are and to send someone for me so I can get home. And *hurry.*"

The confusion was evident on Mary's face, but she by now realized that the situation was dire and offered no time for explanation. She sat at her desk and began punching in numbers on her phone.

Thank you, Mary, I thought. *Thank you for not asking questions.*

The line rang repeatedly in my ear, but no one answered. Broken, feeling like everything had been ripped out of me, I dropped the phone on the hook. I gasped in my seat and choked back a sob that escaped anyway, not knowing what to do. A tear broke loose and slid down my cheek. I wiped at it furiously.

Sam Evans came around the room and began massaging my shoulders. He spoke in a smooth, reassuring voice, trying to comfort me. "Try to relax, Leslie. Sit still for a minute and breathe deep, get your head."

I closed my eyes and did what he said, inhaling long and hard. I kept my lids shut for a long time and saw countless images superimposed on themselves in the darkness.

Christ, I can't believe this has happened ...

I heard Mary's firm voice across from me, speaking into her phone. "... that's right, yes. We're at the Reformed Church on the corner of Main and Fifth, and we're snowed in. Our vehicles are snowed down in the lot. Yes. Okay, thank you."

I heard her hang up, and I opened my eyes to see her.

Her eyes were bright and brimming. I saw hope shimmering there. The first sign of hope. She said, "The police are on their way to your house, and they're sending a unit here. I was told they'll be here within ten minutes."

I nodded nervously, chewing a nail with ravenous fear.

"We'll go with you," Sam said behind me, still massaging my shoulders. "Mary and I."

"Thank you," I whispered in a choked voice, nodding.

My mind was still racing, trying desperately to reconstruct the entire picture and accept it as true.

Still can't believe this, just can't believe ...

It had never occurred to me that I'd been on the line with little Justin Rudebaker all that time, my next-door neighbor. I'd have never recognized his voice because I didn't *know* his voice. Everything fit now; all the puzzle pieces fell into perfect junction. All that stuff Justin had said about not knowing other boys in the neighborhood was true because Justin almost never came out of his house. The Rudebakers had been our neighbors for as long as I could remember, and that's *all* they had been. Just neighbors. For some reason, I had never acquainted myself with them. The only reason Justin knew our home number was because he played with Patrick on occasion, but that was strictly on occasion because Justin was rarely allowed outside.

And the far side of his house, where the laundry room was located—there were no doors on that side because that end of the house overhung the edge of the big hill, below which lay the highway. All their doors were facing *our* home. It all fit now, right down to the nuts, bolts, and screws.

And Justin, of course, had had no idea I was a volunteer at the Call-A-Friend network. And I, likewise, had had no idea he was a caller.

My heart was pounding, thundering. I thought about calling home again, but I knew there was no point in doing so. If Tammy hadn't answered before, she wouldn't now. My blood raced as I could do little more than wonder what had happened in my home. And to think Justin had called *my* house over an hour ago, before he'd called here. His neighbor's place had been *my* place, and no one had answered then, either.

What in God's name has happened tonight?

I quickly related the story to the other five people in the room. I told them how Justin had called and said a prowler was in his home, and how he'd ultimately turned out to be my neighbor. And that no one was answering at my place. They nodded collectively, and their faces grew increasingly distraught.

"I could get home in my Bronco," I said, still sitting.

"Not now," Sam objected, still standing behind me. "It isn't worth risking your life when the police are already on their way. There's eight or nine inches of snow already on the ground out there. The roads are covered, and the wind is blowing drifts everywhere."

"Can *they* even get here, and to my house?" I worried out loud.

"Oh, yeah," Patty Lunesta said, standing next to Mary. "Donald is with the Public Works Department. He says the state cops have these huge Rangers with heavy chains and snow plows mounted up front."

"God, I hope so."

"Just relax," Sam told me. "Everything's gonna be fine. You'll see. You've got the rest of us by your side."

"Want some coffee, Leslie?" asked Luetta in her beautiful, southern voice. I shook my head. I was shaken up enough already. A good dose of caffeine was the last thing I needed.

One of the phones rang across the room, and we all stared at one another. Patty answered, but it wasn't Justin. It was just a girl.

Just a regular, run-of-the-mill phone call.

"Oh, dear," Mary said, "what if kids keep calling in? We have to keep the lines available in case the boy calls."

"She's right," Sam said above me. The concern was palpable in the room. Keeping the lines open meant accepting the incoming calls. You couldn't answer the phone and then tell a child, already in a vulnerable state, that the lines were closed for the night. Only the well-tailored, after-hour recordings could do that.

"Okay," Sam said. "We'll need to keep two lines free at all times. That means just four can be occupied at once. Leslie and I will remain free while the rest of you answer the phones. If it's not the boy, do your best to make the call a quick one. We're all experienced, and I think we can handle it. Are we all on the same page?"

The others nodded in unison. In a deep sanction of my heart, I was thankful that Sam was here and that he was administering some control, some *structure*, to this nightmare. He was a leader, a thinker, and people listened when he spoke. If I made it through this with my son and babysitter unharmed, I'd owe him a tide of thank-you prayers for the rest of my life.

"They should be here soon," Mary said, consulting her watch although a clock was mounted on the wall above the door. I glanced at my Lotensin. It was twenty past nine.

Mary was gnawing her lower lip and gazing past me. "I sure hope—"

Luetta's phone rang. We were all drawn to it like gravity. Her hand fell onto the receiver, and she answered.

Seconds later, her expression widened, and she held the phone up in the air, looking at me.

"It's him, it's Justin."

"My God," I said, hurling my body out of my seat, toward her corner. I grabbed her phone and pressed it against my ear.

"Justin, Justin, are you all right?"

"Leslie?" His voice was trembling. I could tell right away he was crying.

"It's me, Justin, it's me, Leslie. Where are you? What's happened?"

Slow down, girl, easy. Easy ...

"I got in, inside a-around the b-back."

"That's my house, Justin. You're in *my* house. It's me, it's Miss Calloway."

He paused at that but not for long. I wasn't confident he'd wholly registered what I'd said or even who I was.

He continued, "I got in through the back over here, by the kitchen. A window was b-broken, and the door w-was open."

My house *had* been broken into, before Justin's.

A joint robbery. Two houses on one street, on the same night.

The intruders had known of my absence as well as the Rudebakers'.

It was too much, too much to get your hands around—too much to hold onto without losing your grip and your sanity.

I knew Justin was using my kitchen phone because the reception was perfect. He'd abandoned his cordless somewhere.

His voice was shaking violently. "My feet are purple, Leslie. They're *purple*." I could picture the tears pouring down his face in glimmering rivulets.

"Okay, Justin, this is what—"

"I can't feel them anymore, can't feel them at all."

God, I hope he's not frostbitten.

I had to summon all the might in the world not to ask about Patrick or Tammy. The kitchen was at the back of my house. There were two ways out of it—into my living room and off to the dining room, but those exits were blocked off by wooden, swinging doors.

He hadn't yet seen what lay beyond those doors.

"Your feet are numb from the snow, Justin, that's all. Here's what I want you to do. Climb up on the counter and dip your feet into the sink. Plug the drain and turn the water on, *but don't make it hot, or even warm.* That'll burn your skin because you won't be able to feel how hot the water really is. Make the sink handle pointed straight ahead, so it's not hot but not too cold. Then keep your feet in there. Okay?"

"Okay," he answered, and I heard him jumping onto the counter.

"Keep your feet in there and try to wiggle your toes. That'll get the blood flowing in your feet. Soon, your feeling should come back. You understand?"

"Uh-huh. I'm scared, Leslie, I'm still scared. Are those men gonna come after me here?"

"No, I don't think so, Justin. Just stay where you are and stay on the phone with me. We've called the police, and they're coming over there right now. They should be there any minute."

"Okay."

"And Justin?"

"Yeah?"

I bit my lip and forced it out. "Stay where you are until the police get there. *Don't leave the kitchen.* Okay?"

"Uh-huh."

My voice trembled with that last line, and new tears were trying to forge their way through … but I *had* to hold him in the kitchen. For his own good. Although my jackhammering heart tried to deny it with every anguished thump, I knew I couldn't allow Justin to see what might lie beyond those swinging doors.

CHAPTER 14

THE POLICE ARRIVED HERE minutes later. Luetta took the phone and consoled Justin while Sam, Mary, and I bundled ourselves and hurried out to the street where the huge Ranger was waiting. The wind blasted us as we ran, driving powdery snow into our faces. I held one arm up to shield my eyes as our feet plundered through the deepening drifts.

The forecast didn't call for this, I thought as we neared the street. *Not something this bad.*

Emblazoned across the side of the tall vehicle was the emblem of the Connecticut state police. The red flashers were whirling and twirling and throwing bloody stains across the snow-covered street. Seeing those flashing strobes and *knowing* that this vehicle was going to *my* house was enough to sap the strength from my legs. Mary and Sam had to help me step up into the backseat of the enormous Ranger.

The truck was moving before Sam had his door completely shut. A final serpent's tongue of wind screamed through the opening and was snuffed out seconds later when he pulled the door closed.

The driver was alone. He turned partway around to acknowledge us. The near half of his face was bathed in intermittent blotches of red as the strobes jumped off the harsh snowscape around the Ranger. In those initial moments, his indifferent expression was revealed, then concealed in shadows, then revealed again …

The trooper was black. When he spoke, his calm, smooth voice reminded me of a steaming mug of cocoa on a cold and blustery day.

"Miss Calloway, folks, I'm James Trenton, with—"

"What have you heard?" I blurted. "Is my son okay? Have you heard anything?" I was sitting bolt upright in the backseat, between Sam and Mary. Each gathered my near hand in theirs and squeezed gently. The contact was warm and reassuring, but my heart was jabbing at my chest. I was scared. *God, I was scared.*

"Our men haven't arrived at your house yet," the trooper replied, facing forward again. He shifted gears, and the Ranger thrust ahead. His voice was dominated by the grating plow as it ground against the street surface. From the corner of my vision, I saw snow cascading to the right, hurtling through the air in huge, white waves. Ahead of us, the road was gone, sheathed beneath a shifting white carpet. I was amazed the trooper even knew where the road was.

"Naturally, travel is slow under these conditions, and many of these auxiliary roads have been shut down for the night. They should arrive any time."

"You know where you're going, I presume," Mary said, raising her voice to be heard above the grinding plow.

"Yes, I do," the trooper answered—I'd forgotten his name already—without turning around. He remained hunched over the wheel, one hand on the knob of the stick shift. I could see only the backside of his cheek, illuminated by the pulsating red flashers.

"I don't want to hear anything over the radio," I said. "I don't want to hear about Patrick that way. I want to be there."

"Don't worry, it won't come through the radio," he returned levelly, looking ahead. His head was angled to one side to better his view through the windshield. He was *beaming* with concentration. "We'll be there in fifteen minutes, I'm hoping."

"Sit back, Leslie," Sam suggested, on my left. He tightened his grip on my hand and squeezed my shoulder with his other. "Ease back and hang on. We'll get there when we get there. The man has to drive slowly—"

"I just don't want to hear it through the radio, not like that, not before I can even see him," I cut in, speaking so fast that my words were nearly connected. I was also slurring. The closer we crept toward my house on Westfall Boulevard, the less control I wielded on the words that slid out of my mouth.

"I know it," Sam told me softly. "Just relax, and we'll get there safely."

It was pure superstition, I knew. By waiving radio info and hanging on, gutting it out the entire way there, the mental anguish and torture I endured would warrant Patrick's health. I was really reaching for straws now. Anything, *anything* to give me an edge.

The wind drove millions of icy flakes into the windshield, like tiny asteroids. They sounded like hail as they bounced this way and that, rubbed away by the sweeping pair of wipers.

"This storm is unbelievable, simply unbelievable," the trooper remarked, hunkered over the wheel. His voice was a threaded whisper in the Ranger's interior.

I swallowed hard and leaned my head back. This was the worst of it, this ride, the wait, the icy feeling in my stomach. Unable to do anything but *endure*. I turned and looked at Mary, who looked back solemnly, seeming to mirror my countenance. Her face was deep and warm and loving and hopeful but *concerned*. I often think today that she was as anxious as I was that night, most probably unnerved by the grim prospect of handling me spiritually, helping me cope, if the coming news turned out to be bad.

We were on Orchard Drive, negotiating the hazardous twists and turns I had come to know and respect over time. The snow swept horizontally from left to right across the windshield. The apple trees spread out into darkness on both sides of the road, their branches heavy with snow. Red police lights materialized ahead of us. Emergency vehicles were strung out along both sides of the road. This was the accident scene to which David Block had alluded over the radio. We passed slowly through the middle of it.

"Oh, look." Mary was nudging me, pointing through her window.

I squinted into the darkness and saw a police cruiser on its roof. It had slid fifty feet into the orchard, coming to rest with its back end tilted upward, rear brake lights a pair of crimson eyes unblinking in the forest.

"It was on its way to Justin's house," I told Mary. Sam leaned over, listening. "It's why the police never got there. That's why they never showed up."

CHAPTER 15

WE TURNED THE CORNER onto Westfall Boulevard minutes later. I saw the police presence immediately. Westfall was designed strictly for residential purposes and came to a dead end after the Rudebakers' house. No cul-de-sac, just a dead end with a galvanized guardrail overlooking US Route 7 far below. Even through the swirling wind and snow and the Ranger's wipers, I saw the red emergency flashers from a distance, oscillating through the storm and throwing chaos into the night. That visual confirmation stabbed into me like a garden spade, and I felt my jaws unhinge. As the Ranger rumbled forward through freshly exposed tire trails, I was oddly reminded of ogling similar scenes in other locales at other times. But those emergencies had been happening to *other* people.

I swallowed hard. "Oh my God, that's my house. They're all in front of my house."

I saw Mary turn to look at me through the corner of my vision. For a moment, I thought she'd say, *Of course it's your house, what'd you expect?*, but she didn't.

Sam tightened his pressure on my forearm as we moved closer. His tension was evident through the gesture. The interior of the Ranger fell eerily silent as the scene grew before us. And it did *grow*. Features began to take form, and the stroboscopic flashing gradually originated from more than one vehicle. First two, then three, then four, and then I stopped counting. I saw lights everywhere, red beacons and white lights, headlights and spotlights, then handheld flashlights bobbing up and down in the snowy night, beams slashing all ways through the dark. As we drew nearer, those moving beams became attached to human forms, and I suddenly saw people everywhere. I saw officers in heavy trench coats and other unidentifiable men scooting about the scene in thick, brown garments. Neighbors and onlookers were clumped loosely at the outskirts of the confusion, eyes wide, looking on with morbid fascination. It reminded me of the bridge from which Becky had fallen and all the drivers bending over the concrete railing to see. Disgusted but *fascinated.*

I tried to process everything in a frenzy, my eyes working furiously as we pulled up—but there was too much to absorb, too much happening. I saw the onlookers again and wondered what they were thinking, what they were discussing among themselves. Oh, how *little* they knew.

I saw four ambulances, a pair of Rangers like the one we were in, countless police cruisers, and several other unmarked vehicles equipped with plows and chain-link tires. Men were *everywhere.* Moving in all directions. Some talking, some watching, others moving toward an unknown purpose. What fueled my panic the most was the spatial arrangement of everything; the vehicles seemed to have been parked recklessly, without regard to one another or anyone else. The cacophony of flashing lights was hopelessly out of sync, and as a result the area was rendered in a constant state of pulsing red. The entire boulevard was *frantic.*

Finally, we came to a stop. Sam popped his door open.

"Stay with me now," he said, looking back at me as he stepped out into the snow. "Don't let go of my hand. Mary is right behind you."

I barely acknowledged his words or his caring expression as I slid off the seat, onto the snow-covered road beside him. There was simply too much to take in, too much to keep track of. I heard men's voices, and transistor radios, and Sam's voice beside me, and the hellish wind curdling at my ears, driving sharp particles of snow into the side of my face, making me wince. My heart jabbed fiercely at my chest.

"Come on," ordered the driver, waving for us to follow him.

We plundered through the snow behind him, Sam on one side of me, Mary on the other, as he led us around the front of the Ranger. The big engine was still running, a component of all the background noise, but it was quickly dwarfed by the shrieking wind as we moved away from it. I was spinning my head in all directions, as were Sam and Mary, struggling to obtain a fix on things, trying to lock onto something that looked *familiar*. With the blinding snow and the bedlam and lights and people and voices, nothing about the place seemed familiar at all, not even my own house, which loomed to our left. I saw men walking in and out the front door over there, and lights everywhere.

What has happened here? Dear God, all these people …

My pulse was throbbing at the sides of my neck, pounding inside my ear cavities. I had to squint to see anything at all, and I saw Patrick nowhere.

"Where is he?" I moaned worriedly. "Dear God, where's Patrick?"

"It's okay, honey," said Mary, to my right, clutching my arm. "We're going to know everything in just a minute now. Just stay behind the man."

He led us past the front end of a flashing ambulance, past a pair of conversing officers who paused to give us a speculative eye as we passed, then through a narrow slat between two enormous, unmarked plow trucks that had been parked a foot and a half apart. He turned left, and we followed. The wind was coming at us now, and we all put our arms up to protect our eyes. The snow was hard and stinging as it cut into the exposed areas of our faces. I nearly had to shut my eyes.

We were moving toward my house now, past where the sidewalk should have been, and onto my front yard, calf-deep in snow. I spun my head to the right a bit and saw more activity over at the Rudebakers' house, men milling near the front door. I didn't see Mr. or Mrs. Rudebaker and wondered if they'd returned from their late-night affair or if they planned on returning at all. I saw more men over at the Pattersons' place, fifty yards to the left of my house, and that should have set my mind spinning even more, but it didn't because my brain was overloaded, unable to absorb anything new.

Patrick, where are you? Where the hell are you?

A small group of men was huddled just below my front porch, talking among themselves, and we seemed to be approaching them. Seconds later, the trooper we were following angled off to the right, directly toward them.

Oh God, this is it now. You're about to learn everything that's happened here tonight.

This abrupt revelation unnerved me, and I suddenly had the feeling that bad news was coming. I could taste it in the poignancy of the moment, felt it bulging into the hollow abscess of my throat, and I shuddered horrifically.

Mary turned and looked at me as we approached the group, but I refused to look back. I didn't want to see the fear etched into her face. I could feel Sam rubbing me gently on the back. I think they both anticipated the worst during that moment—I think they tasted the same dark premonitions that I did, and we were equally afraid to learn the truth.

We neared the group. My heart was thundering. *Thundering.* It seemed ready to explode into my throat.

The group disbanded as its members saw us approaching, and a huge man with a gray overcoat stepped forward, distinguishing himself through the torrents of snow that bulled past him. He exchanged a word or two with our driver before approaching us. He stood over six foot, taller than Sam even. His dark hair, littered with snow, was a tangled mess on his head—he was the only one in the group not wearing a hat, I noticed—and he was unshaven. His face was covered with a two-day stubble.

Contrary to his physical size, his voice wasn't booming but was barely prominent over the wind. The cords in his neck bulged as he made the effort to speak.

"Miss Calloway," he said, looking down at me, "I'm Carl Wickman, Chief of Police. I assure—"

"My son, Patrick?" I blurted desperately in a hoarse voice. I felt my entire body go numb beneath the weight of my words. I kept my mouth open to repeat them, but my voice died in my throat, and I was suddenly paralyzed.

"Your son is fine," he said, his expression unchanging. He laid a big hand on one of my shoulders. "Perfectly, wonderfully fine."

I froze for a minute as those blessed words plumed past me. Then I exploded with relief and felt tears sputtering down my cheeks, the wind searing past them, making them feel like ice.

"Oh, Patrick," I sobbed joyfully, weeping as Sam and Mary held me up in the gusting blizzard. "Oh, thank God, thank God, thank ... W-where is he now? I have to see him, I have to—"

"He's fine, believe me," Wickman said, not moving. "He's back in the house right now. I'll have my men bring him out." The towering chief turned to his left and motioned to one of the officers with one hand. The officer nodded and made off toward the front porch and through the open front door.

Wickman turned back to us. "Sorry about having to stand out here. It's best if we stay out of the house until the investigators and forensics arrive." A powerful jump of wind surged past us, and we all paused, tucking our heads down as it roared by. It made a high-pitched whistle in my ears.

"Your son is extremely lucky, Miss Calloway," Wickman continued, stuffing his hands into his overcoat pockets. "It was dumb luck that he slept through everything. He was sound asleep when we got here. Never knew what happened."

"What *did* happen, sir?" Sam asked then, taking the words out of my mouth.

"The house was broken into via a back entrance. Several drawers were left opened in your master bedroom, so we assume it was your valuables they were after, Miss Calloway."

"What about Tammy?" I asked, feeling another knot constricting my throat.

The big man hesitated a moment, peering down at me, and I knew Tammy was gone. "Your babysitter was killed, I'm afraid. We found her on the living room floor. I'm terribly sorry, Miss Calloway, I really am."

A sick feeling found the pit of my stomach, and I felt my legs growing weak beneath me. I swayed and would have fallen had Sam and Mary not been supporting me.

Fresh tears made tracks down my cheeks. I sniffled heavily. "Oh, Tammy, no, not her." I was staring into the ground at our feet, wondering if any night of my life had ever been worse. I squeezed my eyes shut and pressed my teeth together, crying openly. Mary massaged the back of my neck with one hand, trying to console me.

I lifted my head moments later, my vision moist and blurry. The snow tore painfully at the wet corners of my eyes. "Someone's gonna have to … tell her parents—"

"We're taking care of that," Wickman said slowly. "Her parents are being notified as we speak."

I lowered my head and let another sob escape as the horrible image of Mr. and Mrs. Culberson receiving news of their daughter's death entered my mind. The bitter truth burrowed into my core, and I bent forward in the blizzard, crying loud and hard, my knees wobbling. In effect, my muscles went limp, and my body collapsed. I tried to fall forward, but Sam and Mary held onto me as I grieved.

Tammy's parents were presently receiving the worst news a parent could bear. It could as easily have been Patrick, so damn easily. It got inside me and clawed at my soul, making me more scared at that moment than at any time before.

Tammy had been murdered in my home. My Tammy, so sweet, so innocent, who looked after Patrick three nights a week.

Mary hugged me hard, and I wept into her neck. I was a bundle of whirling emotions. Was I to thank God for sparing my child and claiming Tammy? Was I to thank God for anything, really, when it seemed implausible that He'd played any role in this terrible chain of events tonight? It was difficult to know what to think.

The wind whipped, and I heard a voice behind me.

"Mommy!"

My ears pricked, and I withdrew from Mary's grasp. I whirled around, and there was Patrick, bound in a thick wool blanket, standing six feet away. His face was reddened by the flashing lights, his body silhouetted by the porch lights behind him.

"Oh, honey!" I yelled, kneeling in the snow to embrace him. I held my arms open, and he ran to me and wrapped his own arms around my neck, burying his face into me. I whispered into his ear and held him tightly, rocking him. "Oh, Patrick, you're okay, thank God you're okay, thank God." I closed my eyes and held him. "I love you, honey, I love you."

He spoke into my ear. "I love you too, Mommy, but I'm scared. What's happening?"

"It's a long story, honey, it's a long story. I can't tell you right now."

He pulled back to look me in the eye. His eyes were large and confounded, brimming with a child's fear. "What happened to Tammy, Mom? What happened to her?"

I felt my heart pounding and knew I had to tell him, right there and then. "Tammy was killed, Patrick. Some bad men broke into the house after she put you to bed, and they killed her. I'm sorry."

His face contorted, and I grieved for him. He was six years old and so damn confused. He buried his face into my neck again, and I held him.

"Have you heard what happened?" Sam asked Wickman, who was still standing in front of us.

"About the phone call and all? Yeah," he said, nodding. "Enough bits and pieces of it from the Rudebaker boy to put the puzzle together."

"How is Justin?" I asked, looking up from my kneeling stance.

"He's all right," Wickman replied, rubbing his stubble with one hand. "A bit shaken up and all, but he's fine. We're still waiting for his parents to return, wherever the hell they made off to. They may find themselves in hot water after this one."

"For leaving him alone like this, I hope," I said.

Wickman nodded. "Neglect is every bit as serious as physical and sexual abuse."

"Absolutely," Sam added, with Mary nodding in agreement beside me.

"What about those men?" I asked. "Did you catch them?"

The chief shook his head. "Gone when we got here. Must've heard the Rudebaker kid making his break or else the sirens. We found faint footprints leading out the back door, but they were snowed under beyond that point. We think they made for the highway down the hill, probably had someone waiting."

"Route 7 is open tonight?" I remembered the bus accident. "Tonight? In this?"

"Sure, yeah. Plows running back and forth down there, and it's a major road for this area. They'll have it open all night."

"So, they're gone then," Mary said dismally, visibly shivering in the gale. "They robbed two houses and killed a girl, and they're just ... gone."

"As of now, until our team runs its investigation through the three houses, yes. We'll have to wait and see what turns up."

"Three houses?" I asked, standing up, and I suddenly knew.

Wickman was nodding. "That's right. We made our check, and it turns out your other neighbors were hit as well. A three-point job."

"My God, the Pattersons," I mumbled. "They're in Honolulu."

"Let there be no doubt, Miss Calloway. These guys played their cards tonight. This was no accident. This was planned well in advance. We even think the storm added to their advantage. We have several units combing Route 7, but there's only so much we can do. That's why I can't stress how lucky your son was tonight. And the other boy."

I held Patrick against me and looked at Mary, then at Sam. We were all silent for a moment, the five of us, a silence alive with sound. Not of men's voices and howling wind but of the truthful essence of the evil that had conspired here on Westfall Boulevard tonight, and that other evils of similar natures were as likely to happen anyplace else in the world, anyplace where good and bad struggled to strike a stability in what we know as home.

"You and Patrick can stay at my place for the night," Mary proposed. "It's probably best."

"You're a doll, Mary," I told her. "I think we'd like that very much." The last thing I wanted right now was to be in my house, me and Patrick by ourselves. Not tonight.

"Leslie?"

I immediately recognized that voice and saw Justin standing to Mary's right, bundled in a heavy winter coat. His red hair waved and flapped in the wind. A pair of officers was standing behind him.

"Oh, Justin," I said.

He came forth, and I embraced him as well, squeezing both him and Patrick into my arms.

He let go moments later and looked at me, snowflakes blowing past his ears and cuffs.

"You did real fine tonight, Justin. I'm really proud of you. I really am."

"I'm proud of you too," he said, and hugged me again. "Will you wait here with me until Mom and Dad get back?" he asked in the embrace, his voice cracking.

I patted him on the back with one arm while holding Patrick against me with the other. "Of course I will. God, of course I will."

EPILOGUE

July 23, 1994
Dear Leslie,

I helped grandmom today. She has a garden with plenty things like tomates and punkins and berry and eggplants inside with lots of windows for sunlight. A little snake was in plants and grandmom was scared and ran into the house get something so she could kill it. but I got it with my hands and took it out from her plant house to let it go away.

It went away real fast to its hole where it lived it was neat. Grandmom is scared of snakes but says she hates snakes when they always get in her plant house like that.

Cork hates them to. we played trucks at his house after lunch he has big dumper and the dirt mover. I have a bulldozer and steemwheel one to make it flat, our town is Holland. It was Cork's name because he says his dad went there once on a airplane. We made tunnles for the water to go throuh when it rains and a dam in the lake so the people there can fish there when it finished. I talked to dad and we can see a basball game when he comes to see us. Grandmoms dog is Barker but he does not bark too much only when the door bell rings in the living room. Can Patrik come here some time and play trucks with me and cork and see Barker?

Sincerely,

Justin

PS—Holland is almost done.

*   *   *

Dear Leslie,
(July 19, 7:35 p.m.)

Better late than never, right? Sorry it's been so long, but things have been rather hectic. You know, settling in, getting my life in order. I'm sure you can identify with me, whatever you're doing right now.

Funny, isn't it? Neighbors for that long, and you were just the woman next door, vice versa for myself, no doubt. I still remember the day you and Richard moved in, when Pat was still an infant, if you can believe that. Kind of ironic, what it took to get us together after all that time.

I think about it often. We have a small creek that winds past the house out here (an outflow of the Wapsipinicon, I think), small enough to call your own, but wide enough for good thinking. I walk the narrow trail that follows it with Mom's dog, Barker, every morning before breakfast to get my thoughts straight, and I think about it often. It's hard to get on paper, really, because there's so much to think about, and personal feelings that go along with it. It's hard for me to see myself sitting in the fourth row next to Marty, watching *The Music Man*, and imagine what my little boy was going through back at the house, and it hurts to think this. But I'm also thankful in a strange way because at least it made me see things in a different light, in a better light.

That's where I'm most thankful to you, Leslie. I won't go as far as saying that you changed my way of thinking—though maybe you did—but you made me realize a lot of things. I thank you so dearly for that—for enabling me to reach into myself and understand what I found there, and to know what needed to be changed, and for finding the courage to make those changes. Thanks and thanks again.

Marty and I settled our business in court over the summer. I think he was more perturbed by the thought of alimony than that of losing me (a caring sentiment from one of Achulsen's top bacteriologists, right?). I should be shocked, but I'm not, really.

I guess it goes back to what you said about things changing, how you don't notice until things have really progressed—or regressed. When I think about it

*today—while I walk along the creek—I
can't imagine how I tolerated living with
him, especially with all the time he spent
at the lab, playing with his culture dishes
and growing things. And he never should
have kept those things hidden in the house
like he did, as secret as they were. I always
detested that. What if those burglars had
actually found them? Where might we be
today?*

*I'm living with my mother out here,
and things are going well. It's nice to
get away for a while, to get somewhere
different. Mom enjoys the company, I think.
She's lived alone since '84, when Pop died of
lung cancer. We'll wait it out and see how
things go.*

*I'm almost afraid to say it, but I met
someone yesterday. First time, yeah, but
he was extremely polite and attractively
old-fashioned. Can you believe me? One-
time-Sheldon-resident, falling for old
fashions! But that's how it is out here in
this little place that someone got the idea
to call Shellicksville. Harold was his name.
He owns the Corner Market down by
Creekbend (my little creek runs behind his
place). Anyway, I was in there for the first
time yesterday (Mom always insists on
getting the groceries), and I accidentally
knocked some yellow apples off the shelf
and onto the dirt floor, five or six of them.
When I bent down to pick them up (apples
hadn't been on my list), this guy Harold
comes over and insists on getting them*

for me. I tried apologizing, but he said not to fret and insisted I keep the apples at no charge. He even used his apron to wipe them off, then put them gently in my basket. He placed them all in there with their stems pointing upward. Sounds silly, I know, but that's not something you do by accident. It took mental planning and all. He's in his mid- to late thirties, I'd guess, and his fingers were bare, which means nothing really 'cause I just met him, but you never know, right? Jeezum, can you believe me? I sound like a little girl again. But that's okay. It's kind of fun to feel young. Anyway, I think I'll fix up one of my eggplant parmesans and take it down tomorrow to show my reciprocity.

How about you? Another man in your life yet? If not, I assure you that you can feel it again. You'll have to write back and fill me in. Or call us sometime. I've written our address and number on the back of the last page. Maybe you can come out and see us sometime. We'd love to have you and Patrick for a week, seriously. And Justin would love it. I think he considers you an aunt now, if you know what I mean. He always asks when you're coming to visit.

Well, I'll let you go now. Time to get started on that parmesan. I thank you again, for all you've done for us. I think my life is finally getting on track again. I hope your life is going well, and I hope you're still doing what you do best. You have a way with kids and a special warm spot that

knows how to touch people. Really, you do.
Take care, and write back soon.
With love,
Nellie
(8:26 p.m.)

I ARRANGED THE MEMO pages sequentially and slid them back into the envelope. I'm holding the envelope again, running my hands over it. The paper is still crisp and firm but no longer heavy and potent. It seems warm now—warm and light. I feel gratified, really damn fine. I popped some peanuts and gazed across the yard, watching the purple martins.

Things are fine here in North Carolina—not wonderful but fine. We live on an old gravel road that sees only local traffic and an ice-cream truck every day. Mr. Festrada, eighty-one years old, lives three houses down and owns seven golden retrievers. He honey-roasts peanuts and sells them in front of his house. They're delightful. I send Patrick out for a bag every other night or so.

An even older woman lives in a trailer at the far end of the street. Her name is Roberta, and she does these latch-hookings as a hobby. She brought us one the day we arrived, a two-by-three-foot image of a hilly meadow at day's end, in which a lone cow pauses to look into the sunset with a mouthful of grass. Roberta told me she'd worked on it for fourteen months. I was awestruck when I first saw it. It's simple yet deep and revealing at the same time. It's hanging in our living room now, above the television set. I get to looking at it often and think about living on a grassy hillock like that one, pausing to appreciate a mouthful of grass and a beautiful sunset. I'm never inclined to ponder the time before or after that moment in the cow's life, just *that* moment. It's amazing how some of the simplest things can hit you the hardest.

The dwellings here are strictly middle class, if that, and the people are friendly. Even the ice-cream man is a sweetheart. His name is Milo, and he takes his poodle, Winnie, along with him every day. Patrick loves Winnie, and I love the warmth that Winnie brings to Patrick's face. I've already decided to get him a dog for his next birthday.

Patrick and I came to North Carolina near the end of February, five weeks after Justin called me at the church that snowy, stormy night. I can't formulate the words to accurately express why. I think the decision was silently made at Mary's house that night, though I was unable to accept it until several weeks later. My company granted me a two-week reprieve following the incident to regather myself, take a vacation or something, but all I really did was sit in my kitchen and listen to the clock ticking softly above the refrigerator. I did a lot of thinking—a *lot* of thinking—and the more I thought, the worse things seemed to feel. The house grew more alien around me, reeking of the elements that bad dreams are made of: my struggles with Richard, his eventual death and the odd emptiness that followed, the phone call, and Tammy's death.

And Sheldon. Sheldon.

I had a Realtor put the house up for sale. It sold in four days. Sheldon never felt like home again, and I never regained the motivation to return to work as an accountant.

Elsie Patterson lost $12,000 worth of jewelry that night. I lost $7,000, and Nellie Rudebaker lost $21,000. Tammy had been strangled to death with a wire garrote, they told me. They'd found her on my living-room floor, just like Wickman said. I was glad I had confined Justin to the kitchen.

The perpetrators are still at large today, six months later. A thorough investigation produced nothing. No prints or hair or even a snub of rubber from a shoe sole. A police data search turned up two similar joint crimes. One was in

Elmira, New York, two years ago, in which back-to-back-to-back apartment units were entered and robbed. The other was near Savannah, Georgia, four and a half years ago, where four neighboring motor homes in a trailer park were picked clean. No prints or hair or anything was recovered from those sites, either, according to what I was told. It makes you think.

Marty and Nellie Rudebaker escaped allegations of child neglect due to "hazardous weather" that night. They'd gone to see a play in Milford, which had supposedly ended at nine. They'd been swamped by the blizzard and hadn't arrived home until after eleven. Boy, did they get a surprise. Their home had been turned upside down, furniture thrown everywhere, the walls stripped bare.

I was willing to leave Sheldon, but I refused to leave Justin behind on the hot plate. There was still his confession to deal with, and I'm not one for leaving business undone. I considered writing it down on a slip of paper and leaving it in Nellie Rudebaker's mailbox, but that idea was cowardly and full of holes. There was a chance that her husband would get the letter before she did. And even if she did get the letter first, who's to say she would believe it?

Nellie knocked on my door the following afternoon, the twelfth, and asked to be let in. I obliged and even warmed up a pot of tea for us. It was obvious that she'd needed to work up the courage to come see me. Her anxiety showed in the way her fingers quivered when she held her cup of tea as well as the hesitations she employed in her diction. She thanked me for talking Justin through the ordeal, and we eventually got to talking. I won't lay it out for you verbatim—we spoke for over two hours—but as it turned out, she wasn't such a bad person. As our conversation continued and the rapids lessened and the pools deepened, I began to feel touched by the softness in her voice and the tension in her eyes. She was a mother who, as she put it, was made aware of her son's needs and vulnerability by the incident. She confessed to feeling a lot of guilt at the time, for failing to recognize the time being consumed by her job. She had never thought twice about the possibility that Justin might be lonely. This event had opened her eyes, and I was happy for her.

I was able to see an entirely new person in Nellie Rudebaker within those two-plus hours of conversation. The opportunity available, I chose that moment to tell her about her husband and Mrs. Fallon. I told her exactly what Justin had told me and how shaken he had been. Ironically, Nellie wasn't surprised. She made a sardonic face and said she doubted it was the first time her husband had cheated on her. She thought she knew of at least two others, women who worked with the Achulsen Bros.

That was six months ago. I still keep in touch with friends from home: Sam, Mary, and the others. I last spoke with Elsie Patterson in early June, and she told me that Nellie had split up with her husband and that she and Justin were residing with Nellie's mother out in Iowa. Today's letter is my first word from Nellie and Justin since I left Sheldon. I'll write back tomorrow.

Like Nellie, you may be wondering what I do for a living out here, so I'll fill you in. I've learned that accounting is a job that earns a paycheck, but working with children is what I truly love. I've landed a day job at a clinic over in Rocky Mount helping children who come from dysfunctional households. Many are teenagers who come in to be counseled. Teens today need as much attention and guidance as children. Much of my work centers around kids of alcoholic families, but I will occasionally work with teens who have been physically abused. I go to work each day feeling as though I'm making a difference.

I gulped a handful of Mr. Festrada's peanuts and downed the last of my iced tea. It's humid here, but I don't mind. It beats the winter gales of Sheldon.

One thing I left behind, speaking of Sheldon, were my sparrows. But now I have purple martins. If you've never seen a martin, they're wonderful birds, dark and sleek and swallow-like. They winter in South America and migrate up here for the warm season.

There's a martin house near the back of my backyard, elevated twelve feet by a steel pole. Because martins are communal, the birdhouse is actually an apartment complex, two stories high with eight units in each level. Every morning and evening, the yard is vibrant with swooping martins as they hunt for insects. Mr. Festrada told me that a purple martin will eat one thousand bugs a day. A thousand! Now there's a good bird to have around!

Today has been a real cracker, I guess. The birds are out, and the air is sweet. And I got a letter from Justin and Nellie. It's nice to know there are people in the world who still think of you and remain thankful for something good that you did for them. It helps rejuvenate the warm spot in your heart.

I closed my hands around the envelope and smiled in the warm night. It felt nice to smile.

It felt nice to belong again.

ACKNOWLEDGMENTS

I WOULD LIKE TO thank Mark Bauman, Katy Lido, Austin Young, and Shannon Morris. All read early drafts of *The Caller* prior to its original publication in the midnineties. The manuscript has changed a lot since then, but I remain grateful for the wisdom and insight you provided.

And thanks again to Ron Delaney, whose round-the-clock technical support approaches something close to wizardry.

CPSIA information can be obtained
at www.ICGtesting.com
Printed in the USA
LVOW04s1531120416
483256LV00014B/742/P